SHOPPING FOR A BABY'S FIRST CHRISTMAS

JULIA KENT

SHOPPING FOR A BABY'S FIRST CHRISTMAS

by Julia Kent

My mother wants all her kids and grandkids to spend Christmas Eve at her house and wake up on Christmas morning together.

Sounds reasonable, right?

And it would be.

If it weren't *my* mother.

My husband, Declan, is protesting any involvement, though he's openly intrigued by the idea of claiming his territory by having sex in my childhood bed.

And by intrigued, I mean a series of really hot suggestions that make me whimper when I have to say no.

Wait—*why* am I saying no, again?

Mom has turned her house into a Christmas showcase that makes Frankenmuth look like the picked-over clearance rack at Target on December 26. You know those crazy people on Etsy who make felted gnomes out of belly-button lint and use... a certain kind of hair... to make thatched roofs on little decorative elf homes?

Those people are saner than my mother.

There is no force of nature stronger—or more emotionally volatile—than a fifty-something grandmother determined to create holiday memories.

Wait a minute. Maybe there is.

My husband.

CHAPTER 1

"*M*mmmm," I hear myself purring as I open my eyes in the big king-size bed at our Victorian B&B here in the Berkshires. A bed that I can stretch out in, because I smell coffee from afar and Dec isn't between the sheets.

Neither is our seven-month-old daughter, Ellie.

I have the entire bed to myself. I might be married to a billionaire, but when you're the mother of a clingy baby, this right here is *true* luxury.

A whiff of cinnamon accompanies that coffee and now I wonder if I'm dreaming. My naked body rolls against the high-thread-count Egyptian cotton and my legs are smooth. As I stretch, I realize my nipples are free. No one is touching me.

This *must* be a dream.

In real life, there would be a baby babbling "Da da da da da" in tones that either mean happiness, terror, hunger, or plain old pay-attention-to-me-now-because-I-am-the-center-of-the-universe, you-underling.

But not now.

In real life, there are always busy fingers exploring my ears and pulling my earrings and poking into my my mouth when I try to talk on the phone.

And in real life, little teeth bite down, hard, when my milk runs out.

So I must be dreaming, because as I open my eyes, a handsome, hot, endlessly naked man is smiling at me, hair tousled over his forehead as he holds two steaming mugs of coffee and says in a low, happy voice, "You're up!"

I look at the end of his thick, dark happy trail. "So are you."

His smile widens. "Coffee first. Up-ness second."

"Up-ness?"

He shrugs and climbs into bed with me. I admire the muscularity of his legs, toned and strong, curved lines with edges upon edges under tanned skin that is covered with dark hair. "It's up for now. I'm more focused on its in-ness."

"You're inventing words, Declan. I can't understand new words before I get enough caffeine." I bend over him and grab my mug.

He grabs my breast.

"I'm awake!" I squeak, belly moving as I laugh, his body hard and radiating post-sleep heat.

"You thought this was a dream?"

I move as close to him as I can with a hot mug of coffee in my hands. I sip. "I know this is a dream, because this is the best coffee I've ever had."

"High praise from a woman who owns a national chain."

"That cupping class we took yesterday was worth its weight in gold."

His hand moves to my other breast. "Speaking of cupping."

"That joke is so old, Dec. You've used it at least ten times since we've been here."

"Any joke where I can legitimately grab your boob will never get old, my dear."

"We're married. You can grab my boob any time."

"They're usually occupied by a feisty velociraptor disguised as an adorable seven-month-old these days, Shannon. I'm not fighting Ellie for your breasts. She'd win."

"You're comparing our baby to a dinosaur?"

"She hisses. She moves fast. She has tiny arms. She bites." He frowns. "Are you sure you didn't just hatch her from an egg?"

I kick his ankle. "You were there in the elevator when she was born. You think I'd choose *that* over hatching an egg? Give me a dinosaur any day."

Silence is a rare commodity when you're the parents of a baby. We drink it in like the coffee Declan's lovingly, meticulously prepared. The last thirty-sex—I mean, thirty-*six*—hours have been glorious. We're here in western Massachusetts at a coffee-roasting facility run by a company that imports some of the best coffee beans we've found world-wide. Their coffee-making seminars are known in the industry as a must-attend. A perfect confluence has led to this moment:

MOM AND DAD *offered to watch Ellie for two nights.*
 Declan had a business meeting in Costa Rica that was cancelled.
 Ellie started on solid food, so I can leave her more easily.
 We haven't had enough sex.

Now, of all those points, which one do you think Dec fixated on?

The familiar tingle of breasts accustomed to feeding a baby hits and I smile to myself, drinking the last of my coffee. This one is smooth and smoky, with a hint of whiskey at the end. Not real alcohol, of course. I'm learning to discern the essence of fine coffees. Like wine tasting, coffee tasting has its own science and is still largely an art. My palate has become significantly more refined as we forge ahead with our chain of coffee shops, but I still love my favorite blend.

And that drives Declan nuts.

"New beans. Roasted in-house yesterday, single sourced from Guatemala," he says, giving me a jaundiced look.

For all the right reasons. "I still love my Alloy," I tell him, naming my favorite blend.

"How can you do that? How can you drink only one kind of coffee nonstop?"

I pat his naked thigh. "I'm loyal."

"You're rigid!"

I lift one eyebrow and look down at the sheets. "I can say the same for you."

He lets out a grudging laugh. "But when it comes to coffee, you need to expand your tastes."

"Why?"

"Because experimentation is how we're going to stay ahead of the game. The competition is fierce."

"I like what I like. Keep making it high quality and you'll have me forever as a customer."

"You're not our typical customer."

"Maybe I should be."

Given that we work together and live together, you'd think nothing I say could surprise him, but it turns out this

4

is one of those moments where he's impressed. "Maybe you're right."

"Just 'maybe'?"

"I like this," he says, his smile all mystery and challenge.

"Like what?"

"The more-confident Shannon."

"When have I ever *not* been confident?"

"How about the day we met? And, probably, the twenty-four years before that?"

"I was confident!"

"Not like you are now."

"That's true," I grudgingly admit. "I *am* more confident. Have been for a while."

"What made you change?"

"You."

"No. Not just me."

"You started it, though. And I think fleeing from my mother at our wedding at the Farmington Country Club was some kind of turning point."

"It definitely was."

"Becoming a mother, too." I pat my boobs in the universal gesture of *How close am I to leaking?* that all nursing moms have.

A soft, sweet look clouds his eyes, as if he's watching Ellie, but she's not even here.

His phone beeps. "Damn," he says, reaching for it. "Time to get moving."

I lean back against the headboard. "Already?"

"Checkout's in an hour. We overslept."

"When was the last time you could say that?"

"Definitely before May 1." Ellie's birthdate. "And I'll

bet Marie and Jason are eager for us to get back. Watching an infant overnight is no joke."

Especially without the boob, I think, but don't say. Making milk is highly underrated.

"Mom and Dad aren't going to want to give her up. You really don't understand my parents," I *do* say.

"It's not like *you* understand *my* dad." Dec finishes his coffee, twisting to put the mug on his nightstand, the long, taut row of muscle between ribs, leading up to firm pecs and chest hair making me marvel. He's mine. All mine.

"Your father is a hot-air balloon filled with the scent of ego, masquerading as a human being, who sleeps with women three generations younger than he is," I say as I take in the scenery.

Dec nods. "Huh. I was wrong. Apparently you *do* understand my father."

I snort. "And *he'll* never watch Ellie overnight. I'm pretty sure he couldn't keep a Roomba alive without an assistant."

A hand finds my inner thigh, moving up from knees to soft flesh that starts to tingle. It's a hand attached to my husband. The father of my child. My business partner.

And best of all, my best friend.

My friend I get to be naked with.

As he kisses me, I revel in how much more we are to each other than these words that convey specifics. I want the fuzzy boundaries that come from not knowing exactly who Dec is to me at any given time. I need to steep in the ambiguity that normally drives me crazy. I crave unanswered questions and indistinct choices, because it's in the explorative space that we learn who we really are. Who the other *really* is.

Then we learn it all over again as life teaches us that not everything fits neatly into a box.

Declan's body moves against mine, swift and sure, the open spaciousness of the bed, the room, of time itself expanding to meet our needs.

Speaking of things that expand to meet my needs...

Tap tap tap.

"Housekeeping, Mr. and Mrs. McCormick. You said you were checking out at ten?"

Declan groans. "We did? I thought it was eleven!"

"Didn't Dave set all this up for us?" I hiss as I sit up and fumble for the white waffle-weave bathrobe that sits in a messy pile on the floor next to the bed.

"He did. If we're scheduled for ten a.m. checkout, it's for a good reason."

"Or he made a mistake," I say as I pull my long hair out from under the robe's collar.

"Dave doesn't make mistakes," Dec argues.

True. Dave is a dream come true. An even-better version of Declan's long-time admin, Grace.

Don't tell Grace I said that, though. She'd come out of retirement just to prove me wrong.

I open the door just as the maid taps again.

But it's not a maid.

It's a floral-delivery person, holding more roses than a Kentucky Derby arrangement.

"Shannon McCormick?" says a disembodied voice from behind the flowers.

"Yes."

"May I set these down for you?"

"Uh, sure."

The flowers move into the room as Dec shoots me a sly grin. A two-pound golden box of chocolates appears.

"What's all this?" I ask in wonder, turning around to him. Declan has no problem with public nudity. He poses for nude sculpture classes, for goodness sake. Thankfully, he's pulled the sheet over his lap as the delivery person does his job.

"I wanted to end on a high note," Dec says, emerald eyes bright and loving, fringed with dark lashes and an abundance of love.

I look down at the sheet again and clear my throat. "You, uh... managed."

He grabs a pillow and covers the evidence.

I find my purse and start to look for a tip, but the delivery man, a guy a bit older than my dad, with a fringe of grey hair and a charming, happy grin, says, "Your husband took care of it."

"HUSBAND!" Declan shouts suddenly in what *I* know is mock outrage, but the poor delivery guy looks like he's on the verge of a heart attack. "You're MARRIED?" he says to me. "You never said a word while we were chatting on Tinder last night and making plans to meet up here!"

The delivery guy's eyebrows shoot nice and high.

I throw a couch pillow at Dec.

The delivery guy leaves, laughing his ass off.

And soon I'm on *my* ass, under the sheets, the room filled with the scent of roses and the aching sweetness of a final hour to enjoy each other.

And the anticipation of digging into a two-pound box of chocolates on the three-hour ride back to real life.

Declan really knows how to mix business and pleasure.

With an emphasis on *pleasure*.

CHAPTER 2

"*O*kay, okay, I admit it!" I say, exasperated by his needling as we drive to Mom and Dad's house after a final, glorious love-making session that has left me with aching inner thighs, a reminder that sex needs to stop being dead last on my list of priorities in our daily life.

Okay, maybe not dead last. That slot is reserved for exercise.

I grab a maple cream and moan through the joyful noise inside my mouth. "You got me with the flowers and candy. I thought it was Dave's scheduling mistake."

"Dave doesn't make mistakes."

"We all make mistakes."

"Like thinking Dave made an error."

"You get so damn cocky when we have lots of sex!"

Eyeing the platter-sized box in my lap for a split second before returning his attention to the road, he says, "Any coffee creams left?"

"One." I pluck it out and hold it aloft, hostage.

"You wouldn't."

I center it over my open mouth, looking up like a baby bird begging to be fed by Mama Bird.

"Who am I kidding?" he grouses. "You would. You *have*."

"Only when you don't deserve it!"

"I want to try one of the coffee creams to see what the quality's like. I'm sure we can get into that supply chain and probably co-brand. Bring chocolate lovers into our stores."

"Is everything just a business venture for you?" I ask as I grudgingly hand over the chocolate to him. With logic like that, how can I say no?

He pops the candy in his mouth. "You are so easy to bullshit."

His words slowly sink in as I watch him chew.

The grin.

"Wait a minute!" I gasp. "You–you're *not* thinking about trying to work with the candy company?"

His grin widens.

"You *lied* to me to weasel your way into the last coffee cream?"

"I am a master negotiator, Shannon. You never stood a chance."

"Hmmph."

"But once the lie came out of my mouth, I realized it was pretty genius."

"It worked, didn't it?"

"Mmmm," he says, swallowing. "But the idea's not half bad." His eyes narrow as he looks at the Mass Pike, the white line on my side of the car nothing but a ribbon of blur. We're almost at 495, where we'll turn south to head towards Mom and Dad's house. My breasts tingle as I imagine Ellie's face, her soft, smooshie hands, the weight of her little body in my arms, how she smells all cuddled up to me, breastfeeding.

How our eyes meet and all the worlds that came before us stand there, at attention, ready for this moment.

"You're thinking about her, aren't you?" Declan says, glancing away from the road.

"How can you tell?"

His glance darts down at my chest. I pat my breast.

Wet circle.

"Damn it!" I hiss, reaching inside my shirt to pull out a now-soaked breast pad. "These are supposed to prevent that!"

"Oxytocin, right?" he replies.

"What?"

"Oxytocin. It helps release the milk."

"How do you know these details?"

"I read parenting books."

I swoon. No, really–I *swoon*. He's turning me on with this kind of parenting knowledge.

"How do you have time to read parenting books?"

"Audiobooks."

A light bulb goes off. "You listen to audiobooks about babies? When?"

"When I work out."

"You go to that nasty gym with Andrew, Vince, and Gerald, and you listen to books that talk about lactation and babies and *oxytocin*?"

"I do. Sometimes. Other times I listen to business books, or sports memoirs. I know you listen to audiobooks sometimes. What do you listen to?" he asks me.

I blush. Is this the part where I admit all my audio-books are really true-crime podcasts and that I'm a Murderino?

"I listen to social science books related to cut-throat strategies," I say slowly.

His eyebrows go up in an expression of being impressed. "Nice. Which titles? I need to expand my repertoire."

Crap. Can't admit I love *My Favorite Murderer* or *Serial* now, can I?

"I don't remember specific titles," I say, wiggling out of this one. "Ooooh, here's your favorite. Orange cream!" I reach towards his mouth with the chocolate.

"I'm not a big fan of–mmmmmm," he says as I shove it in. Before I can move my hand, though, he bites my index finger.

And holds on.

"Dec!" I squeal. We're racing at seventy-two miles an hour down a four-lane turnpike. "Stop!"

His tongue starts doing unspeakable things to my fingertip. Unspeakable because when he does that, I can't speak. I can only moan.

So I do.

My pulse has been settled back where it belongs, deep in my circulatory system, after being relocated nicely between my legs for the day-and-a-half sexfest we've been allowed to have. It emerges again, taking its place on the queen's throne it rightfully occupies when her king needs her.

This man's tongue should be insured.

Abruptly, he pulls away, the slow, steady push of the car's brake telling me why. I look up and see that he's been paying attention to the road all along, our lane closing shortly as construction forces a merge to the left.

I lick my sticky, orange-chocolate finger and give him a

saucy grin, the throb where my inner thighs meet turning to a whimper.

"Think she'll remember us?" he says softly as the car comes to a halt in the zippered line. Closer to home, on a workday, Declan would be more aggressive. Out here, on our way to get Ellie, he's more pensive. Orderly.

Less wildly controlled.

Yes, that's a contradiction. I know. Aren't the best, most exciting things in life a true contradiction, though?

My chest is so, so wet. "I'm sure she'll remember," I say, pulling on the cloth of my top, fluttering the wet shirt like a surrender flag.

"She'll remember *you*. You're food."

"I'd like to think I'm a little bit more than that to our daughter."

The turn for 495 South comes into view, and then like magic, the slowdown ends, the right lane open again. Dec takes his shot and speeds ahead of a long row of cars, emerging victorious, in the lead as we careen around the exit ramp's cloverleaf and he opens up as we race south.

"Fifteen minutes to Ellie," I say, reaching for his hand. The car is new—brand new—a Tesla Model X Dec insisted we need for its space, given the expansion of our family.

I assume that means he expects more kids.

Someday.

"I could not have asked for a better mother for my child," his choked voice answers. I watch his Adam's apple bob as he swallows, the skin at the corners of his eyes wrinkling slightly. When did it start doing that? The lashes are long and onyx, the same as they were five and a half years ago when we first met.

Five years.

I've spent more than five years of my life with this man.

Almost twenty percent of who I am has been shaped directly, intimately, by him.

And we made a whole human being with my *entire body*—and one teaspoon of him.

There's a joke in there somewhere, but I can't make it right now, because I'm suddenly emotional, too. Dec's not crying, but in seconds I am, squeezing his hand and trying to come up with some eloquent response, some way to mark the moment as special, in that way that everyday conversations sometimes take on great importance in the pantheon of memory.

The scent of breastmilk, sweet and innocent, wafts up from my drenched front. He looks down and gives a half grin.

I follow his gaze and laugh.

"My breasts are ruining this tender, beautiful moment," I tell him.

"Are you kidding? Your breasts are *making* this moment."

I snort, then sniff, the tears right there.

"When your breasts are anywhere, they make the moment, actually."

"You are so weird, Declan."

"Then we're a perfect match."

"We really are, aren't we? We work together. We love together. We made a baby together."

"We're building a family and a business together," he notes.

"Not many couples can pull that off, can they?" I ask, wondering on a deeper level: *Can we?*

"I don't know anyone who is doing what we're doing, Shannon."

"What do you think we'll be like in twenty years?"

He takes my hand and kisses the back of it. "Ask me in twenty years."

"Were your mom and dad like this? Before she died?"

He starts to scoff, but stops, frowning. "I know they complemented each other. Dad did his work, Mom did hers. But they weren't what I'd call partners. Marie and Jason are closer to that."

"My mom and dad don't run a business together, much less an empire like your family's."

"Mom came from money. And that family money carried obligations. I guess comparing your parents to mine is apples to oranges."

"Pretty sure there were long stretches of my parents' early years when they couldn't even afford an apple or an orange." These conversations can turn hard corners, fast, the kind you can only back out of blind. Our backgrounds are so different.

Our love for each other is so similar.

I ache for him with an unrelenting feeling that has become a heartbeat. No, not the one between my legs. It's so much more than that. Connected by Ellie now, we feel like more than two people.

Did Mom and Dad feel this way when they had my older sister, Carol? Did James and Elena feel like this when they had Dec's older brother, Terry? I don't think you have to have a child, or adopt a child, to feel deeply connected to another person. There are so many ways to feel this close to someone.

But this one is all I know, and it is *mighty*.

The last stretch of 495 rolls by in silence, my hand on his, my nipples turning into faucets with a slow leak. We make the turn to my old neighborhood and I feel a rush of adrenaline, an internal wave of glee unmatched even by the anticipation that comes from seeing Declan after a long business trip.

As we pull into the driveway, a quick glance at the clock tells me we've been gone exactly thirty-six hours and twenty-two minutes.

It felt like a week.

Declan's mouth is suddenly on mine, his hand in my hair, palm cupping the back of my head as he pulls me closer. For a second, I worry I'll get his shirt wet, and then I don't care, the bliss of his whole-hearted embrace and the sense that he is everywhere making me surrender.

Just like that, our day and a half away feels like a blink.

How can this man make time change?

"I loved this," Declan says as he breathes against my mouth, our foreheads touching. "I want more time like this with you."

"Me, too."

The front door opens. Mom's head peeks out, her body covered in front with navy fabric, a ruffle of hair visible at the top, which means...

"Ellie!" Declan shouts, pulling away from me, his hand on the car door handle and opening it faster than I can put my tongue back in my mouth.

Huh.

Before I can even twist back into my seat, he's reaching for our baby, lifting her out of the carrier, huffing her head as she reaches up and pats his nose.

Dad looks over at me and gives me a thumbs up.

At least *someone* remembers I exist.

My soaked shirt can be handled later, after I get Ellie settled on the boob and my husband peels himself away. We have plenty of clean clothes in the luggage, because aside from the cupping workshop, I was mostly not clothed at all this weekend, per Declan's request.

"Shannon?" Dad asks as he taps on my window, suddenly there, suddenly concerned. I hunch my shoulders and try to bring the two sides of my coat together.

It doesn't quite fit.

Dad's eyes take in the scene and he gives me the one-fingered gesture for *Wait a minute*. I do, sitting in the car, watching happily as Mom chatters with Declan, who is snuggling our baby.

And then Ellie twists in his arms and stretches her chubby hands out.

For my mom.

·

CHAPTER 3

*S*ome piece of my chest turns in place, twisting hard. The look on Declan's face causes me pain. He's being rejected.

By our baby.

Because she's attached to Mom.

Gracious and mature, Declan hands the baby back. Ellie finds the chunky plastic necklace around Mom's neck and fixates on it. One hand goes through his wavy hair, Declan doing everything he can to manage his emotional reaction. I can read him well. I know how much emotion roils under the surface.

I get out of the car just as Dad re-appears with an enormous UMASS hoodie sweatshirt, the zippered front a relief. I wrap myself in maroon-and-white school spirit as Mom turns to me, holding Ellie out.

"Mommy's home!' she crows as Ellie's eyes get enormous, fixed on me.

And then she dive bombs, like a seagull at a potato chip convention on the beach. Mom barely hangs onto her, my arms reach out instinctively, and the bottom of

18

one of the S's in UMASS gets clamped between her little jaws.

Even Declan laughs.

"Okay, okay," I mutter, unzipping, pulling my wet shirt up. Ellie latches, and I swear, we sigh in unison.

Dad's hand goes to my shoulder as he eases me towards the house. "Let's get you someplace you can sit down and we can bring you some tea."

"I want to hear everything about how it went," I blurt out, the words stumbling over each other. "It was so hard not to call all the time! Did she sleep for you? Was she crying for the breast? Did she eat the peas I left? You didn't give her that awful teething gel you used on Tyler, did you? Was she—"

"We'll tell you everything," Dad soothes as I walk up the steps to the front door, Ellie in my arms. She reaches up and grabs a strand of my loose hair, big eyes meeting mine.

Ah, there it is.

All that love.

How can so much love be pointed right at me?

"She looks happy," Declan says in a complex, layered voice that I can't decipher.

"She is! You two are raising such a happy child!" Mom gushes as Dad disappears into the kitchen and I plunk down in a recliner chair, using my hips and back to pop it into a laid-back position. "She barely cried."

"But she did cry?" Declan clarifies.

"Oh, sure," Mom says with a dismissive wave. "All babies cry. I just let her cry it out. Only took two hours or so. But Ellie was a dream. All you have to do is light a cigarette and rub some whiskey on those teething gums and she relaxes immediately."

I never knew Declan could turn so red.

Dad snorts. I burst out laughing, startling the baby, who pops off, looks around, and latches right back on again. Declan lets out an aggrieved sigh.

"Gotcha!" Mom calls out, pleased as punch. "Declan, I would never smoke in front of her!"

"Or at all," Dad adds. "You quit in 1981."

"I only smoked for a few years."

"A few too many." The argument is well worn. Even Declan rolls his eyes.

"But you didn't say you'd never give her whiskey for teething," I note.

"I swear. We only used your freeze-dried placenta powder you told us to use."

Declan stiffens. "We never gave you Shannon's placenta. It came out in the elevator when she gave birth."

Mom's brow furrows. "Then whose placenta did we use?"

"Mine?" Dad jokes.

"Neither of you is funny," Declan grumbles, shoulders close to his ears, tension from real life seeping back in.

"Maybe we're not, but watching you squirm sure is," Dad says. "Beer?"

"Got a six pack?" Dec asks as he follows Dad into the kitchen.

Mom leans forward and whispers, "Did you two have sex?"

"Why are you whispering?"

"Because it's not proper to talk about sex in front of the baby."

"She doesn't understand a word you're saying. And I'm not talking about my sex life."

"Shannon, honey, new parents don't go away overnight

and *not* have sex. I can tell you did," she answers, smug and self-satisfied. Leaning forward, she adds, "I sure as hell hope you didn't waste an overnight without getting some."

"Mom!"

"What?" she winks. "How else am I going to get more grandchildren? It's in my own best interests to give you and Declan these overnights alone."

"Having you babysit Ellie overnight isn't going to speed up our timeline for more kids."

"So you *are* planning more kids!"

I give her back the same smug smile. "Not talking about that, either."

Dad and Dec come back, both holding beers. I reach for Declan's. He frowns.

"That's mine."

"I like that kind."

"Should you drink when you're breastfeeding?"

"Beer increases milk production."

"You'll drown the baby if you produce any more milk, Shannon."

"Besides," Dad interrupts. "I brought you tea." The scent of raspberry and chamomile fills the air.

"Fine. Tea it is. I'll have a beer when we're at home and she's sleeping."

"She's so beautiful when she sleeps," Mom jumps in. "Have you considered modeling?"

"I already model," Dec says dryly. "For Gerald's class. The one you're banned from," he adds, digging in the knife.

Mom's mouth tightens. "I mean Ellie. She would be perfect for ads and commercials."

"No," Declan and I say in unison.

"Absolutely not," he elaborates.

21

"But there's this talent scout who is married to one of my yoga students and–"

"NO."

Declan's resounding rejection of Mom's idea is an electromagnetic pulse of firm emotion. Dad gives him a look of barely controlled balance, his body language making it clear he agrees with my husband but feels he should also defend his wife.

Who backs down.

Instantly.

"I would never, ever reach out to him without your permission," Mom stammers, the words almost making me bark-laugh in outrage at the lie. She absolutely would. Or, at least, would have.

In the past.

Before Declan.

The Shannon I would have been without him comes to mind, a fully formed version of myself in my imagination: I cringe, I curl my shoulders, I stammer, I agree to things I don't really want. I experience community and love, joy and the feeling of being among my people–but also the sense that I have to go along in order to be welcomed.

Here's what Declan has taught me these last five years: I can be me. I can hold boundaries. The world can adapt to me.

And to my utter shock, it almost always does.

"Of course you wouldn't," Declan finally answers Mom after a thousand-mile stare. Then he grins. "We all want what's best for Ellie."

"I think Mommy and Daddy are best right now," Dad says as Declan sips more beer and Mom gets increasingly nervous. "I remember when you were that small," Dad adds, reaching down to brush a strand of my hair off the baby's head.

Declan's smile turns sentimental.

"Carol was what–four? And we had you. We didn't have a pot to piss in, but we managed to buy this house. Marie stayed home. Remember that crazy newsletter you found, Marie? Wasn't there an ad for it in the *Pennysaver* magazine?"

"What's a pennysaver?" Declan asks.

Dad makes a funny sound in the back of his throat. I can't tell if it's amusement or disgust. Chances are, it's a little of both. "An old, pre-internet way of advertising things for sale."

"Like the want-ads?"

"Yes. You remember those?"

"I'm thirty-four. I'm not in my teens."

"Fair enough. Anyhow, the *Pennysaver* was for really cheap ads. Marie found one advertising a frugal-housewife newsletter called *The Tightwad Gazette*."

"And then the woman who wrote it was on Phil Donahue!" Mom gasps. "It felt like divine intervention. By the time you were crawling, Carol needed preschool and our bank account needed a break."

"You turned dryer lint into firestarters for the fireplace. And figured out that you really only need to use one-fourth the amount of laundry detergent the manufacturer says. I was skeptical, Marie, but that woman was right. Saved us a lot." Dad gives her a wistful smile.

"I did some crazy stuff from that newsletter to save money. Remember, Jason? We found that scratch 'n dent store on the South Shore, with a stale store next door, and it was worth the gas money to buy all that discount food?"

"What's a 'stale store'?" Dec asks.

23

"I'm sensing a pattern," Dad mutters under his breath.

"A discount food store," I explain. "Where you can get squashed bread, or packages that are damaged, or the sell-by date is just on the verge of expiring."

"Why?"

"Why what?"

"Why would you–oh. Like thrift shops?" A light bulb seems to go off in my billionaire husband's head.

"Yes. Exactly," Dad says, clearly simmering. "When you don't have money, you find ways to make something out of nothing."

"We didn't have *nothing*, Jason," Mom reminds him, looking around the living room. "We had this. You made it so we had a home."

"I made it so we had a house, Marie. *You* made it a home." Dad holds Mom's hand and the two look at each other in a way that makes my breath halt in my chest. I look at Dec.

He's looking right back.

We have five years. Mom and Dad have nearly forty. All that time gives you deeper roots.

"I remember couponing!" I exclaim, wanting to break the strange tension brewing in the air. "Dad would go to the stores and get the extra coupon sets from the Sunday newspaper, and Mom would figure out the sales. Remember double coupons?"

Dad groans. "I remember all those gas-station owners who got to know me by name."

"Remember how we almost became newspaper delivery drivers?" Mom says with a laugh. "Just to get all the free-coupon inserts?"

"And the organic applesauce!" I squeal, surprising

Ellie, who stops nursing and struggles to sit up, leaving my nipple out like it's a welcome mat.

Dec reaches for her, and she bounces in his lap, beaming at him.

"How many jars did I buy?" Mom asks.

"One hundred and fifty-seven!" Dad and I say together.

"Why?" Dec asks.

"Because they were free," Mom gasps, laughing.

"Better than free!" Dad corrects her. "Until the manager changed the code in the cash registers at the grocery store, we were making ten cents off the rest of our order for every jar we bought."

"I remember all the applesauce cakes. And cupcakes," I say, memory making the taste tickle my tongue.

"And then there were the deodorants." Mom's a funny shade of near-hysterical pink.

"Deodorants?" Declan asks, clearly unsure whether he should risk it.

"It's a long story. Involves a—"

Dad cuts me off. "We learned that students would dump all kinds of perfectly good stuff in the dumpsters at the local state college when they moved out in May. So one day my buddy Tim and I went to the dumpsters by the dorms, looking. Found some decent things, like working fans, a few lamps, even a dorm fridge. One of those little ones. Kept that—it's my fridge in the Man Cave."

"That's why it has all those Joy Division stickers on it?" Dec asks. "From the college students?"

"No. I just like Joy Division," Dad explains with a shrug.

"Not to mention Beyoncé."

"NO!" Dad practically shouts. "*That* was the college students!"

"Really?" Dec smothers a grin. "Wasn't she like ten years old then?"

"Anyhow," Mom jumps in, covering for a flustered Jason, "Jason and Tim looked in one of the dumpsters. Found an unused jug of laundry detergent. Then a bundle of folded sheets. But Tim jumped in."

"Jumped in what?"

"Jumped in the dumpster."

Ah. Now I know what pure disgust looks like on my husband's face.

"There were all these boxes. Shrink wrapped," Dad continues as he happens to look at Declan. "Like tissue boxes in a three pack. Only these were in cubes. Five high, five deep, five across. And there were so many of them! Lightweight, too. Tim started tossing them out to me. Got four of them and then scrambled out. We didn't want campus police to come after us, so we cut one open to see what was in there before taking anything."

"What was it?" Declan asks.

"Sampler packs for students. You know–trial-size items. Shampoo, deodorants, breath mints. We stuffed the car. Tim sat outside, pulling all the useable stuff out, and we left all the empty boxes."

"Four cubes, a hundred and twenty-five boxes each," Declan muses.

"Right. By the time we were done, we had five hundred of them."

"That's a lot of deodorant."

"Sure was. Took us eight years to use it all. And that's after splitting the haul with Tim."

"Eight years?"

"And it was all scented for women! I still can't smell baby powder without thinking of Jason," Marie smiles fondly.

Dad: the ultimate alpha male.

"All that money we saved made a difference," Dad pipes up, as if someone said otherwise. "Deodorant is expensive."

"You know what I think about all this?" Declan comments. Dad's face goes defensive until Dec adds, "I think it shows the power of teamwork. You know how to find people and inspire them to work with you. And then the two of you worked together to make your family better," he says to Mom, too.

I've never seen quite that look on Dad's face before.

"That is exactly right," Mom says, wiping the corner of one of her eyes as she reaches for Ellie. Her loving eyes meet Declan's. "We are a team. Our family has always been so close. And we really treasure spending time together working towards a common goal."

Why is the hair on the back of my neck starting to stand up?

Declan's head tilts, like he's evaluating Mom, trying to figure out where this is going.

"And that's why we offered to watch Ellie. Because we're a *team*." Her grin is so big, it's like the Moon–if the Moon were slightly crazy and used just enough Botox to smooth out the biggest craters.

"Marie?" Even Dad is on alert. Uh oh. Mom's working herself into a froth here about something.

"We're a team, like the Patriots. Like the Red Sox. Even the Bruins!"

Oh, no. Is Mom about to recruit us to sell mascara and lip gloss that never comes off? She has all those leftover cases of it in the garage, because the company she signed up with went out of business when customers developed chemical burns. Especially after the company started recommending their blush as a labia enhancer.

I shudder as our honeymoon comes to mind.

"And that's why," she continues, her voice high and filled with emotional affect, like one of those coaching monologues in really bad made-for-cable-television movies where the underdog football team is about to take the field, "I want you three to be here with the rest of the family on Christmas Eve. So we can wake up on Christmas morning as the Jacoby-McCormick *team*."

CHAPTER 4

"*H*uh," is all Declan says, a surprisingly understated response to my mother's version of the speech from *Remember the Titans*.

"All of you!" Mom squeals. "Shannon, you, Ellie, and Chuckles!"

"Chuckles? But you have Chuffy and they don't get along." I pause and look around. "Speaking of which—where's the dog?"

"Jeffrey and Tyler are dogsitting. They love Chuffy. Tyler's not scared of him at all anymore."

"You're paying them?"

"No. It's like Chuffy's their part-time dog. Carol won't get them one, so we share ours sometimes," Dad explains.

"And on Christmas morning we can all wear matching pajamas—even Chuckles and Chuffy!" Mom says, clapping like she's on *The Price is Right*.

Declan gives her a look like he's the host of *Shark Tank*.

"Chuckles is boycotting all costumes. Especially the reindeer costume this year," Declan says casually, as if he personally talked to Chuckles about this issue over green matcha lattes and lemon poppyseed cake at one of our coffee shops.

"How do you know?" I ask.

"He told me."

"You... talk to Chuckles?" My eyebrows reach the North Pole.

"No. Of course not."

"*Whew.*"

"*He* talks to *me*. I just listen."

I laugh. Dec doesn't.

"You're serious?"

"Almost."

"You can't be almost serious about a cat *talking* to you."

"You claim Cherry Garcia whispers to you from the freezer aisle at the grocery store, Shannon."

"BUT THAT REALLY HAPPENS!"

Smug arms cross over my husband's chest. "We can *both* be right, you know."

I laugh. "Now *that's* just crazy talk."

Meanwhile, Dad and Mom are watching us like this is a tennis match and Serena Williams just walked out dressed as a candy cane.

"Are you two done?" Mom says primly. "We're waiting."

"Waiting for what?"

"An answer."

"You're serious?" Declan chokes on the last swallow of his beer. "You really want us to spend the night Christmas Eve and wake up here for Christmas Day?"

"I want to see Ellie's widdle face when she realizes Santa came last night!"

Declan whispers in my ear. "Is there a guarantee that

Santa will come the night before Christmas if we do this? If so, that will sway my decision."

I elbow him in the pancreas.

"You can sleep in Shannon's bedroom! We added a trundle bed in there, so there's plenty of room. And Ellie's crib is already there, so it's perfect!" Mom continues, somehow managing to look Declan straight in the eye while he gives her a look that reminds me of a Soviet interrogator holding a skin-flaying machine.

Hmm. He *is* fluent in Russian. And there was that recent article about the KGB planting spies all over the U.S. What if—

"You bring Chuckles here. I'll handle all the food. All the work will be done by Jason and me. Imagine—all you have to do is show up!"

"With Chuckles. In a cat carrier. Driving from downtown to the suburbs. And we have to haul all of Ellie's stuff, her presents, your presents, our overnight clothes and toiletries, and—"

It's Dad who cuts me off, much to my surprise. "And that's all doable." His face goes tender, the smile almost punctuated by tears shining in his bright-blue eyes. "It would mean a lot to us."

Us.

Dad just said the magic word. Not please. Not muzzle (for Mom).

Us.

Fear spikes inside my chest. "Are—is everything okay? Is there something you two aren't telling me?"

"Like what?" Mom demands, hand going over her heart. "What would we hide from you? I share everything with you!"

"No kidding," Dec mutters.

31

"No—I mean—why is this so important? You're freaking me out. Like—is one of you having health problems? Or are you moving to another country? Why is this suddenly so important?" Dad rubs the back of his head, auburn hair streaked with more and more white.

"Because it's Ellie's first Christmas! They only have one first, you know. For everything. And you can control the firsts, but you—you can't control the *lasts*!" Mom wails, suddenly dissolving into tears. Dad puts his arms around her, closes his eyes, and just lets her cry.

I look at Dec and widen my eyes in the silent expression that says *What's going on?*

He gives me back the patented Declan McCormick look that says *I don't know but get me out of here.*

Boy, does he look like Chuckles when his eyes move that way.

"Mom?" I ask, touching her elbow. "What's wrong?"

"My baby had a baby!"

"Seven months ago," Declan whispers.

"MY BABY HAD A BABY!!!" Mom shouts, though her face is in Dad's shirt, so it comes out like a tuba blatting into the wind.

"And that makes you feel... old?" Declan asks, trying so hard to be comforting.

Mom bursts into fresh sobs.

"Stick to being tall, dark, and mysterious," I hurriedly tell him. "And quiet."

"No problem there," he says, taking Ellie and walking out the back door, leaving me with a puddle called Mom and a dad trying to figure out what to do with his hysterical wife.

"Mom, I know this means a lot to you—"

"And me," Dad reminds me.

"But we need to think about it."

Her head pops up, like a meerkat in a hole. "You will?"

"Yes."

She sniffles. "That's more than I thought I'd get. I assumed Declan would put his foot down and say no."

"That's not how it works with us."

She snorts.

"No, really. We collaborate. We make decisions together."

"Like us," she says to Dad. "Jason and I are all about consensus."

If by 'consensus,' you mean Mom railroads Dad on everything until he finally draws a rare line on a major issue, then yes, she's right.

"Good," I say, noncommittal, trying to calm the crazy lady. A quick connection with Dad's gaze confirms I've made the right move. I feel like I'm being trained in hostage-negotiation techniques.

"I think I'm getting old," she confesses. "Declan's right."

I'm so glad he's not here to hear that.

"And when you get old, you think about life differently. You are at the beginning, Shannon. Everything before you is new. You have a new baby and a whole life to live. You don't know yet whether Ellie will be a princess-loving child or a soccer star. Maybe she'll be into anime and go to cosplay conventions, or be focused on money and programming like Jeffrey. Or be quirky like Tyler. Amy's grown up to love corporate life and wants to be a CEO one day. And then there's Carol, who is so relaxed and easy to be with because she seems content and to know herself well. There are all these parts of my life that are fixed."

"What about Shannon?" Declan asks, coming back into the room in time to hear most of Mom's descriptions.

"What?" Mom looks like he jostled her.

"You mentioned every one of your kids and grandkids, except Shannon."

The strangest look comes over my mother as all the pieces of me start to assemble themselves inside my skin, Declan's full attention to *my* needs, *my* existence, *my* acknowledgment giving me a rush of strength and appreciation I consume cellularly.

"My goodness! I did, didn't I? I'm sorry. I guess I was just—because you're the one I'm talking to—I—"

"Middle-child syndrome," Declan says in a matter-of-fact voice.

"What?" Dad, Mom, and I say it in unison.

"Middle child. Shannon's a middle child. So am I. We're the ones who fade into the woodwork."

"You don't fade into *anything*," Dad says to him.

"And neither do you," Mom says to me, remorse in her words. "You have turned into an amazingly devoted mother, a wonderful go-getter in business who still balances a calm, aware life with what could be a high-stress situation. You have your head on straighter than any woman I know."

My throat seizes with emotion. We smile at each other, the querulous grins of people trying to hold it together as sudden emotion takes over.

"Okay," I say, urging her to continue, but not knowing what to do, inside me, with her words.

She sniffs, clearing the moment in a way that isn't dismissive. It's just... we can't handle all that emotion right now.

Plus, Mom has an agenda.

"I get these images in my head, Shannon. I imagine my entire family, all in front of a roaring fire, drinking peppermint cocoa and singing holiday carols. We're all smiling and happy and not a single care in the world is bothering us. No one has an ex-husband calling collect from prison to harass us for money. No one has a thirteen-year-old car that failed the Massachusetts state inspection. No one has an alarming fast-growing cyst on their shin but refuses to go to the doctor because they're stubborn."

Dad looks really sheepish suddenly.

"No one has an IEP that starts to talk about autism again. No one has a vaginal-dryness and labial-tearing issue that her doctor says is a function of menop–"

I hold up my palm. "Got it. Message received. In your holiday fantasy, we all live fairy tale lives where nothing's wrong."

She perks up. "Right!" She laughs. "Maybe that's why I didn't mention you. Before. Because you don't have problems I feel like I have to track, or help with."

"But Mom, life doesn't work that way. We all have issues. Conflicts. Problems. Even seemingly perfect billionaires."

"Not on Christmas. For twenty-four hours, I want one problem-free day. I want the Pinterest fantasy. I want it to be like a Hallmark movie."

"But–"

Perfectly manicured fingertips cover my lips. "Just consider it. Please."

"You're sure you're not dying of some mysterious disease? This is sounding like a dying wish."

"No, honey. Just a massive drop in estrogen and a hip that makes it impossible to do reverse cowboy."

Dad blushes.

"Marie, that's, uh, called reverse cowgirl."

She winks. "What we did, Jason, requires its own, new name."

Oh, yeah. Nothing's wrong with Mom.

She's just fine and normal.

CHAPTER 5

*I*t's two days later and I'm back at work, the overnight with Declan tucked into my memory banks. I miss him. The ache isn't going away, especially since he's on a short trip to New York to deal with some investment bank.

I also miss Ellie, who is back at our place, safe with Mia, her amazing nanny. I'm taking my lunch break for a rare visit with my bestie, Amanda.

Who is telling me all about the finer points of *grout*.

"You have to remember that the color changes after it sets and dries," she mutters around a piece of whole-grain sunflower-seed bread. "And the brand really makes a difference. Any good tile craftsman can work with bad grout, but you can create a real masterpiece with the good stuff."

"Grout, huh?"

"Quality is so underrated." Amanda chews, giving me a few merciful seconds of peace. For some reason, she looks different today. I can't put my finger on it.

I peer at her and say, "I've heard grout is the new dog anal gland."

She gives me a *WTF?* face. "What are you talking abou–ohhh." I'm lucky she doesn't throw a piece of bread at me, but then again, with bread this good, you don't waste it.

"You're kind of going... on."

"Don't lecture *me* about my obsessions, Ms. Organic-Lanolin-for-Chafed-Nipples."

"That was important!"

"So is my grout!"

"Your grout doesn't feed an infant!"

"And your nipples aren't the center of the universe."

"Tell that to Ellie." I sip my iced tea. "And Declan," I add under my breath.

"Remodeling is a pain in the ass. We're so close to being done. All the major systems are finished. Now it's just the tile in the foyer bathroom and then we're really, truly done!"

"You're not redoing the treehouse?"

She freezes mid-swallow, her cup of coffee hovering over the breadbasket. "The what?"

"The treehouse. Doesn't it get an overhaul?"

"Why would we remodel that?"

"For your kids," I tease.

Pink makes her cheeks look adorable. "Um, we're not–it's not–it'll be awhile..." she sputters.

Pay dirt. I knew it!

"You're trying!" I crow. "Aren't you?"

My phone rings. It's Mom. I ignore it.

"Blowing Marie off again?" Amanda asks with a smirk that only someone with a normal mother could pull off.

"Of course. I'm not getting dragged into her newest

yoga thing. And quit changing the subject. You and Andrew are TTC?"

"What's that?"

"Trying to conceive."

"I know what TTC is! What's Marie's newest yoga thing?"

"Pole yoga. And quit distracting me!"

"Pole *what?*"

I sigh. "Pole yoga. She found this pole-dancing studio somewhere north and now she wants to combine pole dancing with yoga." I tear off a chunk of bread and dip it in the rosemary olive oil. "She calls it Polyoga."

"Did you just say 'pole yoga'?"

"Yes."

"Sounds like yoga for chickens in Spanish."

"Don't say that to her. It'll be her next idea." I shudder. "Can you imagine my mom with a bunch of chickens in little unicorn costumes? Making them do downward-facing dog?"

"How does she spell it?"

"P-O-L-Y-O-G-A."

"Are you *kidding* me? That reads like 'poly yoga.' Yoga for polyamorous people!"

I nearly choke. "I never thought about *that*. Great."

"Please tell me someone disabled her Facebook advertising account after the Unicoga fiasco?"

"Dad changed the expiration date on the payment card. He's hoping that will at least slow her down."

Ring! Ring!

Mom again.

Amanda points to my phone. "Get it over with. You know she'll just keep calling. My phone will ring next."

"Why yours?"

"Because she always calls me when you ignore her."

I pointedly shove my phone back in my purse. "Let's see if you're right."

As if on cue, Amanda's phone starts ringing.

I get a smug smirk that makes her look a lot like Declan. "See?" she says.

"Don't answer that. I want to hear more about you and Andrew and the adorable baby you're trying to make!"

She grabs the phone and looks at the screen. Her face changes. "Weird. It's not your mom."

"Who is it?"

"James."

We both shudder. Our father-in-law.

She practically throws the phone on the table and stares like it's an exotic animal. "Why would James call me?"

"He needs a blood sacrifice?"

Her flat evil eye makes me wonder how close to the mark I am.

The ringing stops.

"*Whew!*" she says, echoing my thoughts exactly. "No call from James McCormick's personal number can be good. It's always his assistant. Anything personal is..."

"Creepy?"

"Frightening. It means he wants something from me."

"Like a grandchild?" I tease.

"You already gave him one."

"He wants a male, you know."

"Ellie is perfect!"

"James is a big old sexist, though. Wants a grandchild to pass on the McCormick name."

"Ellie might keep her maiden name."

"Let's not worry about my seven-month-old's marriage

prospects just yet," I tell her, leaning forward. "Let's talk about my mom's announcement over the weekend that she wants Dec, Ellie, and me to spend the night Christmas Eve and bring Chuckles because she has this fantasy that the whole family will be together?"

"That sounds AWESOME!"

"You worry me. Seriously. How can that be awesome?"

"I'm an only child. Christmas mornings were nice with my mom, and Aunt Patty sometimes. But when there's only one kid you open all the gifts from Mom, and then the gifts sent from relatives who use weird wrapping paper. Then it's over, and you pig out on candy from your stocking and hit sugar-coma phase before lunch."

"That sounds AWESOME!"

"Don't make fun of me!"

"I'm not. Really, it sounds awesome. I had two sisters, so Christmas morning was a pink toyfest. And no outside relatives sending stuff, because they were all dead or my parents chose to have no contact."

"We've talked about this before. How Christmas was so different for us."

"Yeah, but I wish we'd talked about it sooner. You only said something our senior year. At least we got you and Pam to come over that one time."

"It was magical," she says with a sappy smile. "So why wouldn't you and Declan want that for Ellie?"

"Because Mom's already talking about costumes for Chuckles."

She winces. "She can go a little overboard."

"A little? Were you at my wedding?"

"I nearly drowned at your wedding."

"BECAUSE OF THE TARTAN DRESS SHE MADE YOU WEAR."

"Poor Chuckles had to wear one, too," Amanda reminds me. "We were a team."

"Because she made him the flower girl!"

"You're yelling, Shannon."

"Of course I'm yelling! You're defending my crazy mother!"

"Now you sound like Declan."

"I take that as a compliment."

We both laugh until we're bent over, almost crying from hysterics. Only long-time friends who are embedded in your DNA can have mood swings like this with you. They enter your inner world and settle down in your spot on the couch, grab your bowl of popcorn and watch you unravel like you're their personal Netflix binge.

Now—watch me do it to her.

"So Declan found out from Andrew that you two haven't done it in your childhood bedroom, and now he wants to beat his brother to it," I inform her.

Her face twists with a horrified disgust. "Your husband wants to have sex with me in my childhood bedroom?"

"No! What?" Wasn't expecting her to make *that* connection.

"But Andrew and I had sex in the shower!" Amanda protests, though one side of her mouth curls up in a satisfied little expression that makes me understand why people say that couples start to look like each other. That is a McCormick trait right *there*. If I sound like Declan, Amanda's starting to resemble Andrew.

We're in Creepyland territory now.

"Yeah," I reply, ready to burst her bubble. "Dec says that's a nice add on, and it gets you points, but it's not the goal."

"The goal? The goal is nailing us in our childhood

beds? They can do hostile takeovers of rival companies, or make small governments change shipping ports for the sake of tourism, but *this* is their goal? THIS?"

I hold up my palms in protest. "I didn't say it made sense."

"Actually, it does," she concedes.

"Sex," we say in unison.

"Men," we add.

"McCormick men," Amanda further clarifies, as if I didn't know that already.

"We always say this when they use us in their competitions!" I complain.

"Because we let them!"

"We don't *let* them. We—we get roped into these messes. It's not like we have a choice."

"Au contraire. We do have a choice. This time, we know what they're up to. We can say no."

"Say no to... sex? Good sex?"

"Great sex," she groans. "If it were just good, it would be easier to turn down."

"That's the problem, damn him. Damn Declan for being so good in bed!"

"Andrew, too."

"Oh, I'm sure Andrew's fine. But Dec is—" I start fanning myself with the dessert menu.

Her finger goes up in the air. "Hold on there, sister. Are you saying Declan is better in bed than Andrew?"

"How would I know?"

"But you just said as much!"

"I'm sure you *think* Andrew is tops in bed," I start to explain, unable to keep the smarmy tone out of my own voice. I clap my hand over my mouth.

Pure fire flames in her eyes. "You did not just do that!"

43

"Do what?" I mumble from behind my hand, knowing damn well what I just did.

The waiter, who has introduced himself as Chip, rescues me.

"The cedar-planked salmon with sage and coconut-milk roux," he says, delivering it to Amanda like it's a trophy. "And the lobster couscous in a caper-lemon sauce."

She's glaring at me over her perfectly grilled piece of pink fish. "My husband is better in bed than yours!" she declares.

Chip turns the color of our white napkins.

"Um, if you need anything from me..." he says, voice so insincere, he reminds me of my ex, Steve.

"We're good," I say, smiling sweetly. "Just arguing over some business details."

"Business?" he asks, clearly regretting his blurted-out question. "What, um—what line of work are you in?"

Amanda's eyes meet mine. Unity comes from the strangest of impulses. We both kick into mystery-shopper mode, the performance more important than our separate egos.

Plus, I'm kind of bored today. Might as well have some fun.

"Have you ever heard of O?" Amanda asks him, taking the lead. Improv isn't just a comedy style. I pivot internally and prepare myself for whatever direction this is about to go.

"O as in…?"

"The O Spa?"

"Oh! *That* O! Yes. You work there?" One eyebrow goes up. He looks like every waiter at every scratch kitchen restaurant in Boston, which means he looks like a dude bro, a hipster, a techie—a guy my age. There is no "type," unless he has sleeved tattoos or wears a suit.

Or both.

Amanda leans forward, unintentionally making her shirt divot in, her cleavage on ample display. "We're testing a new product. Husband swapping."

"Wow." *Gulp.* His throat tremors. "That's a... thing? For women?"

"It could be." She winks.

"And you two are arguing about your husbands,' uh, *performance* because..."

"Because she's trying to claim my brother-in-law is better in bed than my husband," I jump in.

"Brother-in-law? You're married to... brothers?"

We nod.

"I—that's progressive."

"Thanks!" I chirp. "What do you do when you're not waiting tables, Chip?"

"I'm working on my paramedic license. Already a part-time EMT back home. Eventually I want to be a firefighter and paramedic."

"Where's home?" I ask.

"Upton."

"Hey! We're from Mendon!" I say reflexively, the shared smile a friendly, neighborly look that really doesn't square with our husband-swapping joke earlier. I start to die a little inside.

"Nice," Amanda says, turning to her food, trying to end the conversation.

"People really go to the O Spa for things like husband swapping?" he whispers, big brown eyes aglow.

Amanda clears her throat suggestively. "They go to the

O Spa for lots of reasons. Great massages, intellectually stimulating discussion, intense workouts..."

"And the sex-toy store is divine," I add, as if we're talking about shoe inserts.

"But husband swapping?" His ears turn a lovely shade of pink.

"Sorry, Chip. Didn't mean to upset you," Amanda says, though her face says *Sorry not sorry*.

"Oh! Oh, no. Not upset. Just–" He's flustered as a pager on his hip goes off in silent mode. I can hear the low buzz. "I just–you ladies enjoy your meal."

He scampers off.

Amanda takes a bite of salmon, moans, then points her fork at me. "You are so mean."

"ME? You started it! But he's from Upton! He might know people we know! It's bad enough the paparazzi follow us around in Boston. Can you imagine Mom and Dad getting inundated with rumors that we're husband swapping?"

"Marie would eat that up."

"STOP IT! We can't mess with the poor waiter like that."

"You went with it."

"I'm a follower! You can't blame me." I stuff my mouth with lobster couscous like it's a punishment.

It's not.

"Are we really arguing about this?"

"Yes. We've reached James-level ego defense."

She looks mortified. "This is bad! We're becoming..."

"I know."

"McCormicks!" she hisses.

And then we laugh hysterically.

Because that's what besties do.

"You're totally spending Christmas Eve at your parents' house," she says, pointing at me again with her fork. "Especially now that Declan and competition are involved."

"I know."

"And you secretly want to, don't you?" She squints one eye.

"Yes," I confess. "It'll be sweet and awesome for Ellie to wake up with her cousins. This will be the biggest family celebration on Christmas morning since Jeffrey and then Tyler were born."

"That's pretty special."

"Want to come?"

"No."

"Why not?"

Primly, she takes another bite, then just smiles at me. "Because I like to buy tickets to the circus. Not perform in one."

I throw a small breadstick at her. It lands in her cleavage.

We're going to get banned from restaurants soon.

And I don't care.

CHAPTER 6

"We should have left earlier," Declan mumbles as the traffic starts before we even get to the Pike. Red lights glow, surrounding us like a Christmas tree, if it grew into ten thousand cars all headed in the same direction, cluttering the highway and making us fume.

Merry Christmas.

Or, rather, Christmas Eve.

At least Ellie is asleep in her carseat, head slumped forward in that relaxed way babies have, their bodies so calm and trusting. It feels good to know she has that deep sense of relaxation and surrender.

"I wish I were that bendy," I say, looking in the backseat.

Dec's eyes flash to the rearview mirror. "Me, too," he whispers, squeezing my knee.

My attention shifts to Chuckles, his face behind the bars of his cat carrier. Our eyes make contact. He licks his lips slowly, left to right, as if to say, *I am imagining feasting on your left calf after killing you in your sleep for this abomination of a cage.*

"Sorry," I whisper to him. Mom wants Chuckles back home for some crazy reason, one likely involving that reindeer costume Dec was talking about before.

"For what?" Declan asks, staring straight ahead and gripping the wheel like we're in the Indy 500.

"I was apologizing to Chuckles for making him go to Mom's house."

"I'll take one of those, too, if you handing them out."

I sigh. Merry Christmas.

The light changes. Two cars make it through. Traffic in Boston is like a dystopian movie, where the country is divided into zones and someone from each zone has to fight the others to the death. Substitute "turn left on green light" for "fight to the death" and you have our current reality.

And then there are the clueless out-of-towners who seem to require an engraved invitation to make a turn.

"I'm starting to see why Dad always had drivers," Declan fumes as someone with a Kentucky license plate doesn't take their chance and gets stuck in the middle of the intersection two cars ahead, paralyzed with fear.

Or their car broke down.

It's hard to tell the difference.

"What matters is that we're together," I soothe.

"Da!" Ellie says from the backseat.

"Uh oh."

"DA!" she screeches. "DA DA DA DA DA!"

"That's not a happy sound," Declan mutters.

"At least she's not saying–"

"Muh muh nuh nuh. Muh muh nuh nuh."

My breasts tingle.

"Eight months old in another week," he says with a smile. "Her language is amazing."

Muh muh nuh nuh means *Stop everything and nurse me.*

Which is impossible to do in a car that is in downtown Boston, trying to merge onto the Mass Pike on Christmas Eve.

"DA! DA DA DA DA DA DA!" she screeches. Lately, "Da da" means anything from *I love this!* to *Demons are in my uvula* to *Give me the car keys to eat.*

Right now, I'm going with demons, because how dare we deprive her of *muh muh nuh nuh?*

"*MEOWWW!*" Chuckles wails, joining in the impromptu backseat holiday choir.

"This was a bad idea," Declan says, a tone in his voice making me tense up. I know that tone. He's revving up to vent, non-stop, about how we should turn around, go home, pull out of my family's Christmas. When Declan decides that a situation is all about sunk costs, and stopping what we're doing is the best way to salvage whatever can be saved, he will not be convinced otherwise.

But this time, I'm holding my ground.

And casting blame.

What? Isn't that how this works? We've been together for five years. The traditional anniversary gift for that may be wood (and don't get me started on Declan's jokes about *that*), but there's another relationship level that gets unlocked:

Elevating blame to an art form.

I think every couple likes to imagine their relationship is better than everyone else's for at least some stretch of time they're together. Superiority is an innate human trait. Some of us have a deeper need for it than others. I have no illusions that Dec and I are better or closer or at some elite relationship status compared to the rest of the married world, but I do know this:

He is *wrong*.

"This is a great idea! My family has these wonderful traditions. Mom and Dad have had all the grandkids at their house every Christmas Eve and Christmas Day for twelve years, since Jeffrey was born. We're keeping this beautiful family–"

"I get it."

"Why are you ruining Christmas?"

"I'm hardly the Grinch."

"MUH MUH NUH NUH." Ellie's decibel level increases.

"You're being grouchy and grumpy," I say in a sing-song voice. Fumbling through the diaper bag, I find a small bottle of bubble solution and start blowing bubbles, twisting towards Ellie.

She stops screeching, chubby hands reaching up, eyes shining.

"Bub-UH! Bub-UH!"

"That's right!" I gush. "Bub-ble."

"BUB UH," she screeches, wriggling in her car seat.

"Great. Same word, different screaming," Declan mutters.

I burst into tears.

Nat King Cole starts crooning about chestnuts roasting on an open fire and I'm ready to roast something of Declan's, for sure.

"Can't you s-s-see how this is making Christmas s-s-suck?" I ask, anger starting to replace my tears. "We're going to Mom and Dad's for our daughter's very first Christmas. It's supposed to be magical. You might as well be saying 'humbug' all the time, Dec!"

"UM BUH! UM BUH!"

He gives me a flat look that makes him resemble James so much, I gasp.

"Now you've got her chanting 'hum bug,'" he says. "Like I'm Scrooge."

"*MEOWWW!*"

"If Chuckles starts saying 'humbug,' I'm turning the car around."

"You said she's advanced for her age," I say, trying and failing to keep the sarcasm out of my voice. Tears return, salty and filling the back of my throat.

"DA DA UM BUH!"

Dec looks at me, eyes wide.

"Did she just say a—"

"Was that a—"

"*Sentence?*" We ask in unison.

"Ellie's first sentence is *Daddy humbug?*" Declan starts snort-laughing. I've never seen him do that before.

It's contagious. I join in.

That's the other thing about being with someone for a long time: you trust them enough to drop your anger when they show their vulnerable self to you.

Our sweet child, with dark hair like Declan's and wide, brown eyes like mine, holds her fingers out, curling her thumb and extending her index finger. Elegantly, she pokes a small bubble with just enough force to pop it.

Then she claps.

"Yay!" I call out, clapping with her.

Declan's shoulders drop. We merge onto the Mass Pike, out of the snarl, the cars separating like dandelion seeds after a strong gust.

"Dada um buh buh buh."

"Three words! She's a genius!" Declan says in a low, proud voice, stretched by a huge grin on his face. I don't think that was three words, but I'm not arguing right now.

I put my hand on his knee and squeeze. "Almost eight months ago I pushed her out of me in an elevator. And you caught her."

"One of the best days of my life," he says, voice filled with emotion.

"It was a bit of a mixed bag for me,"

He laughs again. "I'll bet."

"But she's worth it."

"Of course." He clears his throat. "So are you."

"Worth being tortured by Christmas Eve and Christmas Day with my mom?"

"Absolutely."

"MUH MUH NUH NUH!"

Fortunately, I came prepared for this, breast milk in a sippy cup. Ellie just started using one a couple of weeks ago and, to our surprise, she took to it like a champ. The reach back makes my shirt hike up, cold air blasting my midriff.

Ellie greedily latches onto the cup's top, rhythmic sucking noises filling the car.

"I should still sit back there with her," I tell Dec, who gives me a half grin. The buttons for the car's heat are in front of me, begging to be pushed. Pulling my shirt down, I let my body re-warm itself.

And then I change my mind and jack up the temperature in the car.

"She must be cold," I say, turning around again, rescuing her blanket from the floor and laying it on her again.

Ellie kicks it right back off, feet wiggling furiously, eyes right on mine as she does it.

Go ahead, Muh muh, those eyes say. *Make my day.*

My kid has already figured out Newton's third law of physics. The one with an asterisk, for parents:

For every item thrown on the ground, a parent will retrieve it.

"She's fine." His eyes jump to mine. "You really are a great mother."

"I try."

"You don't just try—you succeed."

"Thank you." At least once a week, he says this to me. I still don't know where to put it in my emotional library. Being praised for being a good mother feels like being handed an award for taking out the garbage, or washing dishes.

Isn't this just what you *do?*

"I couldn't have chosen a better woman to have my spawn."

"SPAWN? You make them sound like little devils. Minions."

Now we're laughing again.

Declan reaches for the dash and scans until he finds a station with more contemporary holiday music playing. The unmistakable opening cords of a Trans-Siberian Orchestra song come on. Nostalgia washes over me, the kind that only music can elicit.

The visor mirror gives me a view of little Ellie. The sucking sounds have disappeared. Her eyelids are drooping.

"Turn it up," Declan says to me, but I shush him with fingers placed on his forearm as he reaches forward.

We have a signal we've created between the two of us to indicate when Ellie is falling asleep. I hold my thumb and index finger up an inch apart, and slowly close them.

He nods and goes immediately quiet, withdrawing his

hand from the dash, settling back into driving, a satisfied smile joined with the distinct release of stress from his shoulders.

"Success," I whisper, a heavy metal guitar mixed with Tchaikovsky turning the air in the car into a witches' brew of cheer.

"You did it," he says with an appreciative chuckle.

The highway is full of fellow travelers, all headed to their respective gatherings. Red taillights form uneven patterns in three parallel lanes. So far, everyone's going just under the speed limit. The traffic is so thick, we don't have any other choice.

"I'm sorry," Declan says. He shakes his head slightly, as if annoyed with himself. "I shouldn't have been so negative.

"That's okay," I assure him. "It's a stressful time."

"I don't need to add to your stress," he emphasizes.

Conversations like this feel like microsurgery on our marriage, the tiny back-and-forths having significant consequences when I look at the long haul. Imagining a future of negative moments and handling each other's emotional flow takes patience. Perspective.

Vulnerability.

It's easy to get defensive.

It's so hard to stay real.

"Or her stress, either." His eyes dart up to the rearview mirror and settle back on the road. "That's not the kind of father I want to be."

Declan's being *real*.

"Good," I say, joining him in his raw openness. "Because you're not. You never have been. Being negative isn't one of your flaws."

"I have flaws?" he says to me, deadpan. "Why haven't you ever mentioned this before?"

"Oh my, my," I joke, hand going to my neck, lips pressed together, eyes wide, as if we're at a church coffee hour and I've let my *actual* opinion of someone slip through my veneer of social shallowness. "I suppose someone should have told you at some point in your life. It must come as a terrible shock to you."

More laughter.

This is what Christmas Eve should be, I think to myself as all the cars slow down, the approach to Route 495 clogging up the lanes. Declan takes the exit to go south, a well-traveled route that always helps to prepare us for any time we're spending at my childhood home.

Rituals come in different packages. We tend to think of them as larger, ceremonial moments: Waking up on Christmas morning to find Santa's brought presents. Singing "Happy Birthday" to celebrate someone's entrance into the world, or at least the anniversary of that entrance. Carving the Thanksgiving turkey, stuffing yourself to the point of broken pants buttons, and pumpkin pie eaten straight out of the dish with forks and laughter.

But rituals are just markers for emotion. They remind us how to sink layer by layer into another state of connectedness. Every mile that the car travels takes us closer.

Not just to Mom and Dad, Amy and Carol, Jeffrey and Tyler, but closer to a feeling, closer to an experience that indelibly weaves us together, a cloth of family–tighter, thicker.

And now–*bigger*. Our family is growing.

Twelve years ago, Jeffrey was the first baby in the family since Amy. I remember how excited everyone was to have his first Christmas at Mom and Dad's. Sharing in that experience gave us each a little piece of something new, something warm and without words; a memory to put inside us that we could turn to and smile, even in dark times.

It wasn't about giving the baby a giant stuffed panda bear or buying a slew of clothes in the next size up. It wasn't about laughing as Chuckles tried to eat a feather angel that Amy had made in second grade. It wasn't even about Mom's failed pistachio fudge that somehow Dad turned into the best warm sauce anyone had ever had poured over chocolate ice cream.

It was about belonging.

We turn onto 495 and Declan finds his way into the left lane, opening up on the final stretch to the Mendon exit. Our daughter is sound asleep in her car seat in the back, oblivious to the fact that she's about to be the newest baby to share a part of herself with all these people at my parents' house, and I realize I belong in two places.

I'm blessed with belonging.

Openly crying now, I turn to Declan, whose attention is grimly focused on avoiding the speed demons and the confused out-of-towners. Pawing through my purse, I find a crumpled pack of tissues, very battered but still available for its intended purpose.

"Are you crying?" he asks, sniffing as if he's teared up in sympathy, too.

"Yes. Are you?"

"No. It's the end of that cold."

"Need a tissue? I just used this one. All I have left are Wet Wipes, or maybe there's a coffee napkin in here?" I hold up the purse.

"Uh, no. I'm good. Thanks."

His rejection doesn't faze me. I know what he thinks about my purse.

It's where good intentions go to die.

"Did I upset you that much?" he asks as I wipe my eyes.

"No. The opposite. I'm just thinking about all the past Christmases in my life and how wonderful they've been."

His demeanor changes, closing up, closing in. I know that he hasn't been blessed like me. Money? Sure. Local fame? Absolutely. Power? Plenty of it.

But *belonging*? That's one area where my entire family is so much richer than any McCormick.

Bee-boop!

The electronic sound breaks me out of my reverie.

"My phone battery just died," I hiss, looking over my shoulder, hoping Ellie didn't wake up from that–

"MAMA MAMA MAMA MAMAAAAAAAA!"

–sound.

"*MEOWWW!*"

"MAMAMAMAMAMA."

"Is she imitating Chuckles?" he asks.

"Either that or she's negotiating a hostage release with him. Not sure which."

"We're really close," Dec says. "No traffic on this part. Ten minutes, max. Plug your phone into the charging dock."

"But my phone doesn't work with those charging things. I need a cord."

"That's why I said you should upgrade it!"

"But I like my phone!"

I'm too tired to argue about it.

"I'm sure there's a charging cord for an iPhone somewhere at your parents' house. Give her my phone to play with in the meantime."

"You know the pediatrician said screens are bad for children under two. Why would I give her your cellphone to play with?"

Shifty eyes meet mine. "Right. Bad idea. She should never be given a cellphone to distract her."

I squint at him. "You didn't!"

"What?"

"You've been giving Ellie your cellphone to play with?"

More shifty eyes. "Only for very short spurts of time, to help her stop crying."

"DECLAN!"

"MUH MUH NUH NUH MUH MUH NUH NUH MUH MUH NUH NUH!!!!"

"I wonder if there's an app for that."

"No app will ever replace a breast!"

"I'm sure some porn company has, actually," he says in that dry, logical business voice of his.

"Don't talk about porn around our baby!"

"PUH! PUH!" Ellie repeats. "PUH! PUH!"

Laughter pretending to be deep coughs pours out of my husband.

"Oh my GOD!" Pure revulsion pours over me, like realizing the "rain" at a concert is really coming from the guys in the nosebleed seats recycling their beer without making the long trip to the men's room. "No!" I gasp to her.

Which makes her do it even more.

"PUH! PUH! PUH!"

"You're really good at teaching her new words, Shannon."

I hit him. Hard. Wouldn't you?

"I'm driving! Don't punch my shoulder. You'll run us off the road."

"None of this is funny! Quit laughing!"

"PUH PUH!" Ellie says, then lets loose a long flow of giggles, followed by a loud fart.

Which just makes Declan laugh even more.

Searching the diaper bag for her favorite toy, a blue octopus she loves more for the nubby ring attached to one tentacle than for any aesthetic or comfort reason, I ignore him.

I find it and hand it off to her.

"Ah ah ah!" she says. I unclench. Hearing her say her version of *octopus* is way better than porn. I'm leaving *that* word out of the pediatrician report for her upcoming visit, thank you very much.

"I see she's developed the McCormick sense of humor," I say pointedly, settling back into the front seat.

"Porn and farts? Sounds about right. For my brother."

Eye rolls don't get more epic than mine.

"You're going to blame it all on Andrew?"

"Of course!"

"Speaking of Andrew—he and Amanda are on their way to Hawaii for Christmas."

We both shudder, the word *Hawaii* evoking visceral skin memories of our honeymoon.

"Good for them," he says, eyes taking in a small traffic jam at the exit leading to the main road to Mom and Dad's house. The car slows just as the rain turns to something close to snow, but not quite.

"White Christmas forecasted?" he asks.

"I assumed you would know."

"Why would I?"

"Doesn't Dave give you a weather report every day?" I

reach up and grab my hair at the base of my neck, pulling it forward, over my right shoulder. Long, brown, boring hair, but it's mine. Lots of it fell out about a month after having the baby, but it's coming back in slowly, making the crown of my head look full, robust. The ends are limp and raggedy, a reminder that I need to get a trim.

Or shave it all off. Ellie's ripped enough of it from the roots over the last few months to make a full wig.

"He doesn't need to. I have an app that aggregates important information."

"Like what?"

"Weather. News. Stock prices. Terrorism."

"Terrorism?"

"In areas where we buy coffee, yes."

"I think I'd rather talk about porn than terrorism."

"PUH! PUH! PUH!"

Declan snickers. "You can't blame me for this one."

I punch him anyway.

And thank Kris Kringle that Mom and Dad's house is just six minutes away.

I catch Chuckles' eyes in the rearview mirror. They reflect the taillights of the car ahead of us.

Chuckles the Red-eyed Curmudgeon is stuck in a cage next to a baby chanting the word *porn*.

"Still better than living with Marie, right?" I say to our cat.

So help me God, I swear he nods.

CHAPTER 7

*C*hristmas has a scent. It's different for every person, but I'll bet you know what I'm talking about. Maybe it's the way you can breathe in pine and evergreen, so deep it takes you back to when you grabbed a freshly cut Christmas tree by the trunk, smack in the middle, and pulled it out from the leaning lineup of potential candidates.

Maybe it's the giant jar candle that comes out, reeking of cinnamon and allspice, soot ringing the dirty glass with the residue of happy times as you set the flame aglow once again.

Maybe it's the roasting turkey or ham, the whiff of potato-scented steam that comes up from the cauldron in the kitchen as your grandma makes mashed potatoes for twenty.

With a big grin on her face underneath that stern scowl.

For me, it's none of those.

For me, it's grated nutmeg.

"Welcome!" Dad says in a loud, boisterous voice filled

with hearty cheer, the cup of warm eggnog in his hand, waiting for me, cinnamon stick in place, a healthy sprinkle of nutmeg on top. Yes, *warm*. I like it the way I like it and I make no apologies. That's how Christmas works: you do *you*.

Dec is holding Ellie, who reaches for the stick.

Dad glides in like Fred Astaire, moving to preserve my yummy treat.

I get one last glance at the yard, which looks like someone bulldozed their way through every department store's post-Christmas, ninety-percent-off sale and put all the decorations on Mom and Dad's front lawn.

Which is exactly what happened, come to think of it.

Inflatables dominate, bright lights glowing out of a snowman, a set of reindeer pulling a sleigh, Jolly Old St. Nick, and... a skeleton in a suit.

"Dad?" I point.

He sighs. "Jeffrey insists. It's from The Nightmare Before Christmas."

"Oh."

My eyes take in the spectacle of the Jacoby family grounds, the vision very different from the equivalent of being backstage. Over the years, Mom and Dad just keep adding to the deals they found, nothing ever culled because "It's a Christmas decoration! That's from 1998 when..."

They can't let go of anything that represents family.

"Wa dah. Wa dah," Ellie says.

"Water?" Dad guesses.

I'm pretty sure that's not what she's saying.

"Wa DAH!" she shouts, finger pointing at my drink.

"Another two-word sentence! Want THAT!" Declan says with glee. "So much better than Daddy humbug."

"But less accurate."

He swats my ass as I grab my drink and take a sip.

Carol appears, holding a ceramic Christmas tree with glowing lights embedded in its branches. Centering it on the side table, she looks at me. "Enjoying your glass of warm, spiced semen?"

Dad starts choking.

Declan turns red.

Ellie giggles.

It's Dec who recovers first, bouncing the baby on his hip, turning her around so she faces everyone and away from him.

Leaning in, he whispers to Carol, "If she's going to enjoy warm semen, it won't be in a glass."

Never seen Dad do an impression of a tomato before.

"You may be adults," he says in a low, pained voice, "but give a guy a break. You're all her age, in my mind," he adds, pointing to Ellie.

"Then Dec and I are only here because of a rip in the time-space continuum," I tell him, reaching up for a hug.

"Can we activate that to escape at some point?" Dec asks as Mom comes running over, blinking like a row of police cars got into a brawl with a tow truck and a stoplight.

"ELLLIIIEEE!" she squeals, plucking my baby out of Dec's hands like he's a thief.

"Hi, Marie," Dec says drolly.

"Hi, Mom."

"How's my baby?"

"Good," I say.

"Not you," she snorts, holding Ellie up high, blowing raspberries into her tummy.

"You've been replaced," Carol whispers.

"I've been dethroned."

We laugh.

"Besides, I'm not the baby," I remind her. "Amy is. Where is she?"

"Running late. Some important meeting at work."

"On Christmas Eve?"

"She works for the big guys in finance now. I'm guessing they don't make family time a priority."

"Speaking of big guys in finance, what's James doing this year for Christmas?" Carol asks us.

"Same thing he does every year," Dec replies.

"Eat whiskey-soaked thirty-year-old strippers flame-roasted over a pit manned by even younger strippers?"

"How'd you guess, Carol?"

"Just lucky, I suppose."

I give them both a flat smile. "St. Bart's, again."

Dec nods. "Hamish has another meeting in Boston and Dad's taking him on the plane tomorrow out of Worcester." *Shrug.*

"Why Worcester?"

"Anterdec only has one jet now, and Andrew commandeered it. Dad got mad and hired some private company. I don't know. I try not to pay any attention to those details," he says as we move in a small herd, gravitating towards an enormous spread of cookies on the dining table.

"Must be nice."

"Nice to what?"

"Compartmentalize like that."

A genuine grin makes his eyes light up. "It is." We've been married long enough for him to know not to add, *You should try it sometime.*

"Meanwhile, I'm trying to reason out why James would spend a week at a clothing-optional resort during Christmas, and why in the world Hamish, of all people, would want to see James naked!"

Amy happens to walk in the door as I'm pondering *that*.

"Beer?" Dad asks Declan, rescuing him from a conversation about his nude father. The gratitude on Dec's face makes me laugh as the two of them head to the kitchen.

"Hamish is going to a clothing-optional resort? Figures. He's nothing more than an uncontrolled impulse on two legs," Amy cracks as she gives me a big hug.

"Careful," I whisper. "It's starting to get obvious."

"What's obvious?"

"Maybe you need a big old walking impulse in your bed."

"SHANNON! You sound like Mom!"

"What's wrong with sounding like me?" Mom asks.

Everyone—and I mean *everyone*, including Ellie and Chuckles—laughs.

"I need a drink." I announce, ignoring a glowering mother whose face matches my cat's right now. Chuckles has jumped up onto the staircase banister and is looking down at Mom's new-ish dog, Chuffy, like George R.R. Martin evaluating a wedding to write about.

Chuffy barks twice, startling Ellie, who looks down and says, "Duh! Duh!"

"That's right! DOG-EEEE," Mom says, giving me a pleased-as-punch look. "We worked on that word the whole time you and Declan were on your coffee trip!"

"You have a drink," Dad says to me softly, pointing to the eggnog in my hand.

I laugh. I sip. I relax.

Christmas Eve at Mom and Dad's house has its own rhythm. It's a tempo I would recognize anywhere, like a catchy tune embedded in your life's memory banks from hearing it over and over again.

The cadence of action on Christmas Eve seeps into my bones, making them move with sheer delight through motions I don't have to think before doing. As we move into the kitchen for libations, I look around. Decorative candles rest on nearly every flat surface in my parents' home. Mom will freely admit that she's a bit of an addict, and by 'a bit,' I mean the woman freebases scented-candle wax. There's a famous candle factory out in western Massachusetts that might as well be Marie Jacoby's Mecca.

Like the program for this evening's activities, the pilgrimage to the annual clearance sale at the candle factory is as much a part of our family's rituals as "a pinch to grow an inch" on your birthday, a clementine in every Christmas stocking, or folding towels in thirds because Mom and Dad's first apartment had a shelf above the toilet that required you to fold the towels in thirds to fit, and they still do it out of habit.

In other words, no one questions what we've all come to accept, because this is just how we do things.

Over the years since I've been with Declan, I've learned to look at my family's behavior through new eyes. Not the jaded green eyes of my husband, but something close, minus the negativity.

"Muh muh nuh nuh," Ellie says softly. I take a seat at the table, pull up my shirt, and settle her in, my eggnog waiting for me to drink the rest. Dad put the tiniest hint of rum in it, so little that it won't matter to the milk. Later, when she's asleep, I'll imbibe more. Maybe. There are no rules or rituals around that. The me who has a baby at Christmas is new, feeling her way through darkness to find the glowing light of a path. I make it up as I go along.

Right now, watching Mom pull out the brass angel candleholder, I smile, remembering my four-year-old self and how I burned my fingertips on the hot metal. Ellie is dangling from my right arm, her own fingers prying the very same skin that I injured as a small child. It pains me to imagine her burning her chubby little fingers, and yet there's a circularity to it.

I laugh as Mom unearths handmade ornaments from thirty years ago, starting with my older sister Carol's creations. There's an entire box filled with carefully tissue-wrapped treasures, assembled by little hands that followed teachers' instructions in classrooms where the holiday crafts were an annual tradition. Silver glitter still clings to cardboard sleighs made of egg cartons with pipe-cleaner runners; clothespin reindeer with googly eyes still sport their crooked antlers. The treasures accumulated over the years.

They would, with three children.

And now *I'm* a mother.

Ellie pops off the breast as raucous laughter comes from the living room. "DA DA DA DA DA!" she calls out. I sit her up in my lap, pull my shirt into place, then stand.

What Carol, Amy, and I have always poked fun at suddenly seems touching and profound. What I used to dismiss as a trash-worthy craft from my seven-year-old self now represents a moment in time that can never be recaptured. Mom holds onto these, not just because of tradition, and not simply because of sentimentality, but because each one represents a version of her.

A version of *us*.

Each ornament is a specific marker in time. Excitement is fused into wood pulp and felt and glue, magic preserved in the physical object itself. When we gaze upon it, complex neurological processes take us back to a part of ourselves that we can only access by touching the paper that chubby hands once struggled to hold, by stroking a fingertip along the line of cracked paste that was, years ago, wet and laden with possibility.

Dad and Declan come to the dining room, both holding cups of hot cider.

"No beer?" I ask Declan, who gives me an even look.

"It's still early. I'm pacing myself."

"Here we go!" Mom interrupts, people clearing out of her way as she walks into the room carrying a huge, flat box with various bags filled with something soft. I catch one with my name on it, written in black Sharpie. "Pajamas!"

A confused look from Declan comes my way. "Pajamas?"

"Remember? Family tradition. We all put on matching pajamas."

His eyes go flat. His face goes slack. He turns to Dad and hands off the cider. "Where's your Scotch? All of it."

"Come on, Declan! Look at this!" She pulls out a onesie, red and white striped. Flipping it over, she shows us. "There's a snowflake on the butt!"

"I refuse to wear that!" he declares in a loud, deep, firm voice. Eyes like the blade of a knife lit by moonlight cut through my mother.

Carol doesn't even try to hold in her laughter.

"That's for Ellie," Mom chides. "But now you've given me an idea. Wouldn't it be cute to order these in adult sizes next year?"

"No." It's not just Declan who answers.

Mom ignores everyone and hands the bags off. Tyler wiggles through the crowd, snatches his bag out of Mom's hand, and disappears, thumping up the stairs like a Christmas ninja. Chuffy follows at his heels, tail wagging.

I gleefully take mine and Ellie's from Mom and start for my bedroom.

"Here you go," Mom says to Dec, who takes his bag like Mom just handed him a used Kleenex from an Ebola patient.

"Come on!" I goad him.

"I was serious when I asked your dad where his Scotch was. I need that first before I put these on." He peers in the bag. "Long johns? Not even flannel? Is Marie trying to kill me?"

"They're warm, stretchy cotton. They're festive."

"I'd rather go naked."

"You do know that 'chestnuts roasting on an open fire' is a line from a song and not a family tradition, right?"

Eyes narrowing, he just watches me, intelligence flickering behind those beautiful heather-green orbs. "Maybe I *will* go naked." That's no idle threat, coming from him.

"You can't!"

"I absolutely can. I have no problem being a nude model in Gerald's sculpting class."

"That's not the same."

"Why not?"

"You would seriously boycott Mom's family tradition by going naked? You realize she takes, like, 500 photos."

"I don't have a problem with that, either."

In a rare moment of borrowing one of my mother's character traits, I ignore him and walk upstairs into my childhood bedroom.

Justin Bieber greets us from the wall.

"PUH!" Ellie says, kicking her legs hard.

I ignore that, too.

Dec is on my heels, walking into the room as I set her on my made bed, undoing her outfit as she wriggles.

The piece of clothing he pulls out of his bag is like a fabric candy cane, only green and white.

"Oh, boy," he says, holding it by two fingers like it's a dirty diaper.

"What's mine look like?"

"What do you mean? Aren't they all the same?"

"Sometimes she dresses the boys and girls in different colors."

"I am neither a boy nor a girl."

"You are a Grinch."

He shakes his head. "Can't argue with you there."

"Good. Then green suits you. That's his color."

"Why are all the grouchy guys green? The Grinch, Shrek, Oscar the Grouch..."

"Matches your eyes."

He gooses me. I laugh. I finish dressing Ellie and hand her off to him.

Mom has purchased all the cotton pajamas in the right sizes, washed them, folded them, and even scented them with an orange-and-clove sachet. A moose on a tiny pillow that smells like the Maine countryside, stuffed with balsam and something else, is tucked inside my bag. I shake out my shirt, reach for the hem of the one I'm wearing, and pull it off.

Dec leans against the edge of my desk and settles in for a show.

"This isn't a striptease."

"It's the closest thing I get to one these days."

"Take me to a tapas bar and maybe we'll find another one."

Rich laughter greets my words as we both remember

71

our Vegas wedding escape. "I like you topless better than I like tapas," he says, the words sounding so similar, they might as well be the same.

Which is what got us into that mess in Vegas.

"If I'm topless, she has more claim to the boobs than you do." I point to Ellie, who is sticking her wet finger in Declan's ear.

He ducks to avoid the baby version of a wet willy. "I know. I'll have my turn again," he says with so much warmth and assurance, I want to make love on the spot, just to be closer to him. The feeling is less raw passion and more a deeper comfort. A knowing.

A feeling of being known.

Quickly, I finish dressing, pulling the stretchy, legging-like pajama bottoms on. "Mom did it again. Perfect fit," I exclaim, ever surprised. "How does she manage it?" Ellie's outfit is the right fit, too.

"Satanic spell?"

"She's not that bad."

A hearty sound of disagreement comes out of him, reminding me of his Scottish roots.

My turn to watch his striptease. Button by button, he unwraps himself, better than any present under the tree. These days, our lovemaking is a hurried affair, driven by Ellie's sleep schedule, yielding to a more businesslike approach. We both undress quickly, fall into bed, have a perfectly enjoyable time, then pant in the dark as if we crossed a finish line, aiming for a personal best.

Which, um... of course we do. The best part.

But there is no alluring unveiling. No touch of his hands on mine, peeling me out of my socially acceptable covering.

"Enjoying the eye candy?" he asks as I drink in his

thick chest, the dark hair a joyful sight, his skin less tan than usual but always hot as hell. In five years, my body has changed–pregnancy will do that–but his has only aged in fine, fine ways.

Better than ever.

"I am."

"It's always here for you. You can lick the sugar whenever you want."

"You're making this porny."

"PUH! PUH!"

I bare my teeth at him.

His eight pack curls in with laughter. "Yet again, can't blame me this time."

"Where's the doggy?" I ask Ellie, whose wide eyes turn to catch mine, as if she needs to understand me before looking for what I'm talking about.

Then she looks down.

"Duh! Duh!" she says.

Deflection achieved.

Loud music blares from downstairs, instantly quieted with the turn of a dial. Melody from *The Nutcracker* floats up, making Dec smile.

"My mother played this."

"On Christmas Eve?"

"All through the season. I've told you."

"She loved Tchaikovsky?"

"She loved all kinds of music. She's the reason Andrew's such a Yes freak. Dad never liked her modern tastes. But during the holiday season, she was a traditionalist."

"I think we all are."

"Maybe." Nostalgia changes his face as he looks at the baby. "She would have adored Ellie." Yearning, quick and harsh, fills his eyes until I see him turn away, shoving whatever he's feeling back into the box where it belongs.

"Ellie would have loved her, too," I say, my hand splaying flat over his bare chest. The steady drum of his heart pulses right in the center of my palm. As he breathes, I try to absorb some of the ache he's feeling through my own skin. If I can share the burden, it won't feel so hard for him.

Hit by a sudden wave of selfishness, I feel like crying. "Is this too much? Being surrounded by all my family? The goofy traditions and the feeling that a Christmas craft store threw up all over the house? Is–am I asking too much of you?"

Kind eyes meet mine. "No." Taking my hand off his chest, he turns it over, kissing the knuckles near my wedding and engagement rings. "No. Not too much."

"But it's a lot to handle."

"Mostly your mom is. Not the Christmas stuff. It's nice. I've spent years with your family."

"Only on Christmas Day."

"It's fine."

"If it's not, we can–" His lips stop me, warm and seeking. Letting the kiss take over, I shift Ellie further away on my hip, enjoying the way so many parts of my life bisect.

Until she bites me.

"OW!" I call out into Declan's open mouth, the feeling weird.

"Did I hurt you?"

"*Owww!*" Ellie bites down even harder, my shoulder burning. The shouting from me makes her finally stop, her big eyes meeting mine as I frown and say, "That hurt Mama!"

She bursts into tears.

Wails like I've broken her little heart come rolling out of her, the sound mingling with the pain in my shoulder until the surprise of it wears off and I'm instantly filled with remorse.

"Oh, baby, I'm sorry," I say, pulling her in for a hug.

Rigid muscles from her make that impossible. Her little hands reach for Declan.

"DA DA DA DA DA!" she cries.

I hand her off just as Chuckles nudges open the bedroom door, climbs up on my bed, and curls into a ball of triumph on Declan's striped pajama top.

"It's okay, baby," Declan says in a soothing voice that makes every part of me light up. "Mama is fine. You just can't bite people like that. You're not a vampire."

"I beg to differ," I say under my breath, plucking the cotton cloth out. She didn't break the skin, but those new baby teeth are sharp.

Ellie gives me a vulnerable, shocked look, eyes sparkling from fat tears lining the edges. I rub her head, the uneven dark hair coming up with static electricity.

It makes me smile.

She mirrors me.

"Ma ma," comes out of her, softly, with a final, hitched little breath that says she's done crying. Her eyes move to the bed. "Kih."

"Did she say 'cat'?" Dec asks, moving so she can see Chuckles better.

"Buh kih."

"Bucket?"

"Blanket?"

"BUH KIH!"

"Bad kitty?"

Chuckles looks at her through slitted eyes that cast more shade than a politician's wife meeting a rival.

"What did Chuckles do to her?" he asks me.

"No idea." I reach down for Dec's top, rolling Chuckles off it. He ignores me, too, and sits there, a twenty-pound lump of King Cat.

"Here," I say, shaking the shirt free of cat hair. "Sounds like someone's getting ready for carols." A few piano notes drift up the stairs.

"Carol's already here," Dec replies as he sets Ellie down on hands and knees. She promptly crawls over to the trash can, which is, thankfully, empty.

"Not Carol. Carol*s*. Christmas carols."

He freezes, arms up in the sleeves, about to pull the shirt over his head. Ah, what a pose. The fire downstairs isn't the only thing heating up in this house right now.

"We have to *sing*?"

"Of course! It's tradition!"

Ellie knocks the trash can over and claps for herself, looking at us as if to say, *See what I did? Give me my gold medal.*

Flesh show over, Declan finishes pulling on his shirt. I burst into laughter at the vision of my husband in horizontal green and white stripes, green piping around the neck and cuffs of his pjs. I'm in red and white, and so is Ellie, with a big white snowflake on her butt.

"What's so funny?"

"You look like a piece of hard candy."

He grabs my hand and puts it on his crotch. "I could give you something to lick."

"DEC! Not in front of the baby!"

"She's playing in the trash. We don't matter to her right now."

I twist and look down. "There's no trash in there. She's staring at her porny father."

"PUH! PUH!"

"*GRRrrrrrrrrr*," I say, lowering my voice quickly, afraid to scare her.

Declan laughs as he adjusts himself, turning away. "Look what you did to me."

"What *I* did to you? You put my hand on it!"

Carol pops her head in, tapping on the door, her order of operations ridiculous. If she's asking permission to enter the room, she's got it backwards.

"Mom wants Ellie for pictures," she announces, walking past Dec, who turns away without a word.

I hand the baby off.

Carol winks.

"You know," he says, making sure they're both gone, pulling me in for a hug, his now-hard candy pushing against my inner thigh, "we still haven't had sex in this bedroom. Or even in this house."

The closeness is calming. Safe and alluring. He cages me in with strong arms covered in festive colors, our bodies wearing tight pajamas. The feel of him against me like this so appealing.

"Not happening, bud," I say, letting him down bluntly. "Ellie's bunking with us." I pointedly look at the crib.

"We can be inventive. There's the bathroom. It has a lock on the door. I checked."

"The bathroom? No. Remember the last time we had a quickie in the bathroom at home? When I slid off the sink counter and ripped the toilet-paper holder off the wall?"

"We did that," he says proudly.

"Well, *we* didn't have a scrape on our inner thigh that went so high that it burned when *we* peed for a week."

"Does it still hurt? I could kiss it and make it feel better," he whispers in my ear, using his tongue and breath in ways that drive me wild.

"Dec," I rasp, my throat tightening, knees tingling.

"GRANDMA GOT RUN OVER BY A REINDEER!" Tyler screams as he barges right on in, so excited, he's jumping up and down in his green and white jammies. "GRANDMA GOT RUN OVER BY A REINDEER!" Carol's behind him, laughing. She looks like a vibrating candy cane.

My baby is plunked on the floor. Ms. Snowflake Butt crawls to the trashcan, resuming her anthropological study of detritus.

"Your mom has a real reindeer here?" Declan shouts, gaping at me, hands on his striped hips. "Is she crazy? Wait. Don't answer that. *How* crazy is she? A real reindeer?"

"There is no real reindeer, Declan."

He winks at me, looking remarkably like my sister.

"GRANDMA GOT RUN OVER BY A REINDEER!" Tyler repeats.

"Does that mean we don't have to sing?" Dec asks me, looking as excited as Tyler for a moment. "If Marie's going to the hospital, I mean." He pretends to care.

I punch him. "It's the name of a song."

"Ellie is eating the trash can," Tyler informs us before running away.

We laugh.

Until we don't.

Because in the handful of seconds we didn't pay attention, our baby has managed to crush the wicker trash basket I've had in my room since I was nine, and is munching on pieces of it like they're potato sticks.

Ellie looks right at Declan and says, "Da da!"

Horrified, he reaches down, pulls the pieces of wicker out of her mouth, picks her up, and marches downstairs, half laughing and half stoic. I don't know how the man does it, but he manages both emotional reactions at the same time.

I follow.

Laughing.

CHAPTER 8

*M*om turns on the tart warmer she's placed on the mantel, the living room filled with decades of memories from Christmases past. Instant cinnamon fills the air. It's an olfactory process that makes the room seem bigger suddenly, the scale changing as I remember all those Christmas Eves when I was small.

"Ma ma," Ellie says, twisting in Declan's arms. He hands her to me with a smile.

My stomach tightens and I lean against the edge of the recliner. Ellie's feet go flat on the top of the chair back, knees and hips almost ready to lock into standing position but not quite there yet. Next year this time, she'll be walking. The thought makes tears spring to my eyes at the exact moment that Declan looks at me. His smile changes to a darker concern.

"What's wrong?" he asks, moving over to stand next to me as I let Ellie push off against the soft chair.

I take my free arm and wrap it around his waist, breathing so deep, it's like I'm taking our five years together into my lungs all at once.

"Nothing's wrong," I say as Ellie launches herself up like a rocket, giggles turning into her fuel. "Nothing's wrong at all."

"Declan?" Mom asks. "Can you find the matches?"

"Matches?" Dad comes down the stairs carrying an armload of Christmas stockings, some old and some newer, ready to hang. "Matches are in the junk drawer."

Declan stiffens. "Please don't make me go into the junk drawer," he whispers in my ear. "Once you go in there, you never come out the same."

"It's not that bad," I hiss at him.

"Jason told me there was a dried piece of your umbilical cord in there," he hisses back.

"She's saving them to have some woman on Etsy make a gold necklace out of them."

"Them?"

"Mine, Carol's, Amy's, Jeffrey's, Tyler's, and — "

"Not Ellie's!" he hisses.

"No. Remember? Chuckles ate it."

"I'm not sure which umbilical fate is worse, Shannon."

"Never mind, I'll get the matches," Mom says brightly.

"You just don't want Declan going into the junk drawer," Carol says to Mom with a laugh as she walks past.

"He hasn't been part of the family long enough to show him *all* our secrets," Mom informs Carol, who just laughs.

"You dodged a bullet," she says to Declan.

He gestures to his striped, pajama-clad body. "No. I didn't."

"I can't believe you actually wore them." Carol's pajamas are red and white, like mine. Mom has all the girls in the family wearing red stripes and all the boys wearing green stripes, although Jeffrey has some objections.

"Grandma, this is really gendered," he announces.

"Gendered?"

"Why do all the females have to wear one thing, and all the males another? What if I want to wear red and white?"

"It's too late, sweetie. I don't have any red and white jammies in your size."

"I don't think this is fair."

"How about this," Dad says, putting his arm around Jeffrey's shoulders, then doing a double take. I realize why he does it. Putting your arm around Jeffrey these days means adjusting to his new height. The kid is about to outgrow some of the adults in this family. He's twelve, on the cusp of puberty.

Or maybe that cusp has been reached and we just didn't realize it.

"Next year, you help Grandma pick out the pajamas. Then you'll have a say." In the glow of the fire, Dad's bright-blue eyes look like cerulean crystals, his auburn hair peppered with new white strands. There is no middle ground—his hair is either a warm, deep amber or stark white. Those aging strands make my throat ache.

Jeffrey's brow folds as his eyebrows go up. "Really?"

"In fact, you can have *all* the say," Declan interjects, giving Dad a meaningful look. "Next year, we'll wear whatever you pick."

A shriek comes from the kitchen, Mom running out with dripping wet hands, her green apron with battery-operated blinking Christmas lights getting wet from her furious wiping. The Mendon fire marshal would have a heart attack watching this.

"DECLAN!" she screams, arms around his neck as he stumbles backwards, losing his balance. "You're coming next year, too?"

"Wait. What?" he chokes out.

"You said *we*! You said *we'll wear whatever you pick* and *next year* to Jeffrey. That's a verbal contract."

Carol starts to snicker. Jeffrey nods.

"Grandma's right."

"I am?"

"She is?"

Ellie paws at my pajama top, which seems specifically designed to be the least breastfeeding-friendly item of clothing on the planet. That's Mom for you: fashion over function.

"I did not explicitly say we were coming next year," Declan says calmly as he peels Mom off him like a Christmas window decal on December 26. "Let's see how this year goes."

"But you *said!*"

"Marie," Dad intervenes. "Quit while you're ahead." Rubbing a spot between her shoulder blades, he seems to know exactly how to get her to back off. Someone needs to tattoo that spot. Put a beacon on it.

Make it glow.

The rest of us need to find her reset button like Dad has.

"You know what else is a verbal contract, Grandma?"

"What?"

"What Grandpa said. Next year, I'm picking the pajamas."

Patting him on the head, she gives him a benign smile. "That's nice."

"No, that's *confirmed*."

"You have a job at Grind It Fresh! the second you turn sixteen, kid," Declan informs him.

"That's in four years, Uncle Declan."

"Too damn long."

"Plus, you don't have a store out here. Only in Boston."

"In four years, we'll have one in Mendon."

"You will?"

"Absolutely." A grim determination sets into Declan's face with the business talk.

"Can we not talk shop?" I ask him.

"What?"

"It's Christmas. Let's talk about enjoyable things."

"Business is pleasure for me."

"How about making pleasure pleasure?"

Hidden by my body, his hand slides down and gives me a caress that warms me from the thighs up. "I love making pleasure pleasurable."

"Dec," I hiss as Jeffrey moves to the table, where Mom is putting out more food, this time a holiday cheese ball and crackers. Tyler's playing the piano, simple notes that seem to be a very off-pace version of "We Wish You a Merry Christmas."

He winks at me, then goes over to the piano, sitting next to Tyler. "Hey, buddy."

Tyler ignores him, plunking out the song with the laborious effort of an eight year old learning to play. He finishes the last note, only then looking at Dec and saying, "Hi, Uncle Declan."

"Hi."

"I play piano now."

"I see. You're doing well."

"I want Declan to play."

I listen, wondering, not really sure if Dec does. Declan didn't have a piano in his apartment when we met. While Mom and Dad made us all take lessons, the only one who can really play well is Amy, who is watching Tyler with her head cocked, the same dopey smile of nostalgia on her face that I have.

"I play a little," Dec answers.

"Play 'We Wish You a Merry Christmas,'" Tyler insists.

"Okay." Declan places his fingers on the keys and goes through the chorus perfectly.

Carol rolls her eyes at me as she grabs a gingerbread cookie from a plate. "Of course he plays piano. *Of course.* The guy speaks Russian, bought you a coffee company, models nude for sculpture classes to raise money for low-income arts programs, is an amazing father, *and* he plays piano perfectly."

"He's pretty perfect," I agree.

"Terry's the one who is the true pianist," Dec calls out. "My mother insisted we all learn to play."

Dad and Mom exchange a look that says they were right all those years ago.

"But Andrew and I can just pick out the basics. Terry's playing was at a professional level."

"Really?" Carol steps away from me, towards Dec. "How is Terry doing?"

"Fine, I guess. We saw him at Andrew and Amanda's in August, but I haven't talked to him in a while."

"Why not?" Mom asks.

He shrugs. "We're not that close."

"Did you have a fight?" Dad asks.

"No. Just... we live different lives." With increasing discomfort, Declan fields the questions.

"You'll see him this week for the holidays, though, right?" Mom asks, deeply concerned.

"No. I haven't spent Christmas with Terry since... well...."

JULIA KENT

"Since your mom died," I say gently, knowing the answer.

He just nods. Ellie is in my arms, kicking. She goes still, picking up on the somber moment.

Dad puts his hand on Declan's shoulder. "You're always welcome to invite him here for any family holiday. He's your brother. That makes him family, too."

My eyes fill up. Declan's are so close to filling, too.

"Thank you." Two simple words. Limitless emotion.

"Let's sing!" Carol says, saving Declan from his own reactions. He gives her a grateful look and a nod.

Tyler plunks the first notes of "Jingle Bells."

And we all join in.

No one in my family has any sense of pitch. The point of Christmas carols isn't to get the notes right, anyhow–it's to be in community through song. Right?

At least, that's what the Jacoby family has always told itself.

Declan has a mellow baritone. I've heard him sing before, at church services we've attended here and there, and along with favorite songs. None of the Christmas selections we belt out here at Mom and Dad's requires tone. We stick to the more boisterous songs, like "Jingle Bells" and "Up on the Housetop."

No "Silent Night" or "Away in a Manger" for us.

Pretty sure we'd shatter glass.

"When do we stop?" Declan asks me as Amy finishes playing "Deck the Halls."

"We sing until the first person loses their voice."

I get a gimlet eye.

"You think I'm joking. You should have been here in 2004. It was brutal."

"What happened?" He humors me.

86

"Vocal strain plus strep throat. Poor Dad."

"Ha ha."

"She's not kidding." Dad reaches for a candy-cane cookie from a platter behind us, his other hand holding a glass of something sparkling and amber. "Took two rounds of antibiotics to clear that up, and I lost an octave of singing voice."

"Up or down?"

Dad laughs. "Can't hit those high notes anymore. It's like my throat got neutered."

Ten more songs and finally, we stop with "Joy to the World." A fitting end.

"I need water," Declan cracks, his voice cracking at the end.

The fireplace is filled with glowing coals as Mom sets out platters of simple food. The big meal will come tomorrow, but Marie Scarlotta Jacoby still nods to her Italian heritage. Seafood for Christmas Eve dinner: shrimp with cocktail sauce, crab dip, bowls of clam chowder, breads and crackers all over the table.

At Easter, Dad's Polish heritage takes center stage with the butter lamb, but tonight, it's all about too much food… and the cookies. So many cookies.

Which come next.

Jeffrey and Tyler ignore everything that doesn't have sugar in it.

Carol lets them.

"Excuse me," Dad whispers. "It's time." Twinkling eyes meet mine, then look at Declan, Dad's finger going to the side of his nose before he turns away and jogs into his and Mom's bedroom.

"What's that about?" Dec asks.

"You'll see."

Mom walks over and beams at me. Ellie reaches for her, so I hand her off, my daughter settling in on her grandma's hip like Velcro. With both hands suddenly free, I do what any warm-blooded woman would do in my situation.

I consume chocolate.

"*Mmmmmm*," I groan at Mom's pumpkin-chocolate bars. "Did you use that new organic coffee-cherry flour in these?"

"And spices from the Shaker village in Maine, of course."

"Love those Shakers!"

"They were abstinent, you know," Mom says as Declan returns to the conversation. "Completely celibate."

Turning instantly on his heel, Declan makes a graceful circle as he pivots out of the conversation, the word *celibate* his kryptonite.

"How," Mom asks, oblivious to my giggles, "did they ever expect to last if they didn't produce babies?"

"They grew by bringing in new believers," Amy reminds her. "And widows and orphans."

"All those women! And hardly any male Shakers," she says. "They must have had to take turns."

"Mom! They didn't have sex! It was part of their religion."

"Who believes in being celibate so that the entire religion literally dies out?"

"Shakers," Amy notes.

"They were good with herbs and spices, but their theology needed work."

"Oh, God," Carol mutters under her breath.

"I could never, ever have converted," Mom adds,

giving Dad, now reappeared dressed as Santa, a big, wet kiss on the lips.

"Pretty sure *that* makes me want to be celibate," Amy says openly, rolling her eyes away from Mom and Dad.

She looks *just* like Jeffrey.

Carol and I look at her, hard, until she glares back.

"What?" she demands.

We're pretty sure Amy's a virgin, but she insists she's not. Doesn't matter, of course, but we're her older sisters. In the Sister Constitution, we're required by law to find something to ridicule her for.

Hissss!

"What was that?" Dec asks, looking down the hallway towards the sound.

"Come on, Chuckles. It's not so bad," Mom croons.

I meet my husband's eyes.

"She isn't," he says. "No."

"Have you met my—"

"HO HO HO!" Dad bellows out.

Three things happen instantly:

1. Ellie, who is on the floor, crawling towards the fireplace as Declan stands behind her, plops up into a sitting position and bursts out crying.

2. Chuckles, wearing felt reindeer antlers, sprints into the living room and takes a flying leap onto Chuffy's back.

3. Mom turns the corner, camera in hand to take pictures. Chuffy runs straight for her and under her feet, tripping her.

TEACHING yoga is a family joke when it comes to Mom, but

I have to say that in this moment, namaste out of the ridicule and appreciate how well she falls. What would be a broken hip in any other fifty-something woman turns into falling-angel pose, followed by corpse pose, ending with Mom on her back, Chuffy on her chest, Chuckles on top of Chuffy, and those damn reindeer ears wagging to and fro.

"Marie!" Dad exclaims. Chuckles releases the poor dog and goes right for Santa, scaling Dad's leg and sinking his teeth into the big black plastic belt around Dad's belly. Without missing a beat, Dad takes off the belt, flings Chuckles into a fig tree near the glass sliders, and helps Mom.

"I'm fine," she answers, her voice muffled. "Thank God for those burpees that group trainer makes me do. I'm bendy, Jason." She winks.

Now I know where Carol got it from.

"Actually," Mom says in a crafty voice that means she's up to something, "I really have to credit the Polyoga I've been doing."

"Pole what?" Declan asks innocently.

I kick his ankle.

"Polyoga. Yoga on a pole."

"Like – the North Pole?" Amy asks.

Carol and I draw our fingers across our throats to get her to stop asking Mom any questions.

Too late.

"No!" Mom says brightly. "Pole dancing and yoga. Yoga in high heels and booty shorts is transcendent!"

"Marie, that's not what yoga should — " Dec tries until I stop him, fingers on his lips as Jeffrey retrieves Santa's abandoned belt, giving Chuckles some major side eye.

"Shhh. You'll just make her talk about it more," I tell Declan, who closes his eyes and nods once.

Amy calmly bends down, picks up Ellie, and kisses her face until she giggles. It's an excuse to ignore Mom.

"Grandma really *did* get run over by a reindeer!" Jeffrey shouts, clearly delighted with himself for the joke.

"Children everywhere have been waiting their whole lives to say that line, kid," Dad says to him, laughing, his white beard separating from his lower lip. He starts towards Mom.

Chuckles jumps down, the reindeer ears now hanging under his chin, the strap over his ears. Stopping by Mom's face, he dips his head as if to say, *Pet me.*

She obliges.

As her fingers stroke his fur, he deftly maneuvers so the reindeer headband pulls off onto her fingers.

Turning, he positions his butthole right at Mom's eye level.

Tail up.

Then he moves with the grace of a 1930s glamour actress, as if to say he doesn't give a damn about any of us.

And screw those reindeer ears, too.

"You're right, Jeffrey" Mom says, laughing and wincing, too, her hip clearly hurt but not broken. "Grandma did get run over by a reindeer."

Carol shouts, "Got all of that on video!"

Merry Christmas Eve, everyone.

Another priceless Jacoby family memory.

CHAPTER 9

"*A*hhhhhh," Carol says as she plops down on the couch, a spiked seltzer in one hand, a chocolate cookie in the other. "Christmas Eve. The calm before the storm." Her hair is loose, makeup all gone, and in the striped pajamas she looks cozy, relaxed.

So unlike her normal, harried state.

The three kids are all asleep in their crib and beds, Jeffrey the holdout, claiming that being twelve meant he was almost a teenager, and that meant he was a pseudo-adult who deserved to stay up.

Carol's *no* was simple and clear.

He grudgingly complied.

"Ellie's language is so advanced!" Carol gushes, making Declan smile nice and wide, sitting forward to hear more. "I don't think Tyler said a two-word sentence until he was three!"

"She said a three word sentence on the way here," Declan says. "Daddy humbug bubble."

"What does that mean?" Mom asks, laughing as she

fixes a piece of garland caught on one of the stocking hooks on the mantel.

"Declan was being Scrooge on the way here and I was blowing bubbles to calm her down and she put some sounds together that Dec swears are sentences," I fill in.

"Don't you? I know she's saying sentences," Declan argues with me.

"She definitely said 'Daddy Humbug,'" I concede. "But I plead the fifth on the rest."

Low, relaxed amusement ripples out from Declan. "No matter what, she's amazing."

"*That* we can all agree on," Carol says with a sigh.

"At least there's nothing to set up," Dad says as he stokes the fire, which is down to embers. Somehow, he knows exactly how to calibrate it. "Remember that year, Marie, when we bought the discount dollhouse from China and there were no directions?"

"Same year we got Carol a bike with broken handlebars." Mom sips her drink, laughing. She suddenly looks twenty years younger.

"We were up until four a.m. making it all work." Dad shakes his head and sighs. "Pretty sure it took a full year for the skin on my fingertips to grow back."

Amy comes into the room holding one of the peppermint mojitos Mom made, sitting on the edge of a recliner, smiling. "Was that the year you created the strict 6:30 a.m. rule?"

"Yep," Dad replies, turning to her, his green and white jammies reminding me of Candyland.

"I am hiring people to assemble Ellie's more complex gifts," Declan whispers in my ear, almost making me slosh my eggnog.

I laugh, then drink up, enjoying the warmth that fills my body.

"This is the best part of Christmas," I say to everyone. "I can't blame Jeffrey. I wanted to be able to stay up late, too, but I had to wait until I was seventeen." I glare at the reason.

"What!?!" Amy exclaims, hand to her heart. "I can't help it if Mom and Dad had me convinced until I was fourteen that Santa was real!"

Perry Como croons Santa Claus is Coming to Town on the stereo system. The rum in the eggnog tastes like maple candy, the alcohol buried by love and an all-pervasive calm that washes over me. I snuggle up to Declan on the couch, our baby fast asleep in the other room, ready to wake up and spend her first Christmas ever surrounded by so many people who love her.

Who needs presents when you have *that*?

I don't answer Amy's joking questions, because I don't need to. This is an old argument, a non-conflict that greases the wheels of family. We're bound by all our shared stories, aren't we? Amy was the reason I couldn't join in staying up, needing to be in bed along with her, to keep up the ruse.

To keep the magic going.

"I love seeing you like this," Declan says, brushing the hair off my face. Our legs are hilarious together, his long, mine thicker, the red white and green reminding me of an Italian flag put in a blender. I run my knee up his thigh and burrow in.

"Like what?"

"Relaxed. Happy."

"I'm happy all the time. Okay, *most* of the time," I amend before he contradicts me.

"Not like this. You're in your element."

"Our element." I sigh. "I love being surrounded by family. I love looking around the room and seeing Mom's Christmas decorations. I love knowing that tomorrow morning it'll be chaos and the kids will scream with joy." I look up at him. "Most of all, I love knowing that this is my life. And that I get to spend it all with you."

The kiss is unexpected. Dec doesn't generally go for a lot of public affection in front of my family, so I'm caught off guard, the taste of his beer on my rum-covered lips a funny dichotomy. So funny I smile. He smiles, too, and soon we're kissing and laughing at the same time, the silliness uncharacteristic of him, but so nice.

"Gawd," Carol says, drawing it out. "Get a room, you two." She throws a garland ball at us, hitting Declan on the cheekbone.

"You two are *soooooooo* cute," Amy says, voice caustic. She and Carol bond over their mutual taunting of me. Nothing has changed since we were kids.

"What's wrong with cute?' Mom asks. "I've gotten a lot of mileage out of being cute!"

David Bowie starts to sing Little Drummer Boy.

No one says a word.

"What about you, Declan?" Mom asks, standing and lighting a series of green taper candles in a pewter train that covers an end table.

"What about me?"

"When you were little, what was it like to wake up on Christmas morning to see what Santa brought you?"

His whole body goes still. So still. Then his shoulder relaxes, followed by his jaw, which loosens as if giving himself permission to remember. The body is the gatekeeper for our brains. We think it's the other way around.

But no.

"We rarely spent Christmas at home," Declan says. I know this, but my family doesn't. "We traveled somewhere special most years. Mom and Dad rented a house for a few weeks, and we spent the time traveling there. Dad would only be there for the week between Christmas Day and New Years' Day. Geneva, Dublin, Prague, Melbourne – you name it. Our Christmas presents came from the local economy. Dad's time there was all about business. Mom really made it feel like a holiday."

"She was the glue," my own mother says.

"Yes." Dec finishes his beer and sets the empty on the table. Arm around me, he rests lightly against my body, lost in memory. "Versatile, Dad called her. Mom could shift into whatever social rules were in a given situation. Hayride? Mom wore jeans and flannel shirts. UN reception for the incoming secretary-general? Mom brushed up on her language skills and was Dad's charming wife. Kids need to learn about the world?" One corner of his mouth goes up as his voice drops. "Mom was there."

"I'm sorry she's not here," Dad says to Declan.

"But she is," I say, holding Dec's hand. "She is. You're making her be with us. I wish I could have met her."

"It makes holidays hard, doesn't it?" Mom says, moving over to sit on the floor next to Dad, by the fire. He puts his arm around her shoulders, her head grooving in perfectly on his neck, like time has worn their bodies to mold to each other. "I know that feeling."

"You do?" Dad jerks his head up. "Celeste was nothing like Declan's mother."

"No. My mom wasn't like that at all. I mean holidays are hard because they remind you of what you don't have."

Dec nods.

I frown. "No! That's not how I feel at all. It's the opposite. Holidays always remind me of how blessed I am!"

Mom and Dad exchange a look, then a fist bump. "Success," Dad hisses.

Carol lets out a snort. "You two have ruined me for relationships."

"WHAT?" Dad, Mom, Dec and I say it in unison.

"No, them," she says to me, pointing to Dad and Mom. "If I find someone who is half as good for me as you two are for each other, I'll be lucky."

"Todd definitely wasn't that person," Amy says.

"Understatement," Dad mumbles.

"I know, I know. But," she says, lifting her glass to Mom and Dad, "to hope."

We hold our rag-tag assemblage of glasses, some empty, most close, to her toast.

"To hope," we all say.

Declan yawns. Dad, Mom, and Carol all follow his lead.

"Your yawn is con – " I say, the yawn catching me. " – tagious," I finally finish.

"To family," he says with his empty bottle.

"I'll drink to that, "Dad agrees.

And then we all float off to bed, dispersing like the ashes that float up from the fire, remnants of something warm and wonderful.

But ready for whatever comes next.

CHAPTER 10

*T*he house is so quiet, it *crackles*.

You know how houses settle sometimes, like older people standing and stretching, their joints popping and re-aligning? That's what Christmas morning sounds like right now.

Except–more.

The snapping is glass-like, with a familiar quality. Declan snuggles against my ass, moving his hips with a slow, relaxed movement that tells me he's doing it in his sleep. Morning wood presses against me.

I sigh. I love morning sex. But it doesn't love me these days.

I crack open one eye. The clock says 2:45 a.m.

Huh. Not morning wood. Just plain old wood. High-quality sexual mahogany, with a long, deep grain and a rubbed finish.

I sit up and peek in Ellie's crib. She's sound asleep. *Whew.*

As I settle back down, a glimmer outside the window

catches my eye. I sit back up, my spine curling slowly, ribs warm under my full breasts.

A gasp catches in my throat.

Ice.

It's an ice fairyland out there.

People think that living in New England means our winters are snow-covered, quaint affairs with red barns and horse-drawn sleighs and hot cider around a roaring fire.

Maybe on the Hallmark Channel.

The reality is grey slush for five months, wearing long down coats that are nothing more than vertical sleeping bags with holes for the feet, a *Hunger Games*-like fight for on-street parking spots that you have to dig out yourself (not that I have to do this now that I'm married to a billionaire—bonus!), numbing cold that turns the lower half of your face into a red-chafed mess, and the beleaguered sense that some snowplow drivers are a special form of sadist hired solely for their fetish-like need to pile snow higher, deeper, and in the exact worst spot on your driveway.

Snow bullies at their finest.

"*Mmmmm*," Declan says in the soft spot below my earlobe, his wood polishing itself against my ass. "Merry Christmas. Did Santa come?"

I laugh softly.

"Because I'd love to. Wouldn't you?" His lips replace his nose, the stubble against my neck making the skin under my ribs zing. That tingling is arousal, the kind that comes unbidden, a purely integrated response that shifts me into another space where my body gets the attention it deserves.

His hand slides over me, my shoulder moving instinctively to fit like a puzzle piece with his body, the kiss lush and warm as the ice outside snaps like a percussion ensemble.

Breathless, I murmur against his mouth as his hand slides up my leg, "You're serious."

He moves his hips just enough to show me he has quite a healthy dose of serious going on. "Of course."

"Where?"

"Here."

"Not with Ellie right there!"

One eyebrow goes up in a predatory gesture that I swear has some kind of magnet in it that makes my knees open.

Pressing a finger to his lips, he climbs off me, the sudden lack of warmth making my nipples tighten.

Oh, who am I kidding?

That's not why.

Taking my hand, he helps me stand, and we tiptoe to the door. Thankfully, it's been oiled recently. No creaking. As we step through the doorway, Ellie lets out a big sigh. Dec grabs the baby monitor from the nightstand and we slip out, like time thieves.

No. We're not stealing time.

We're orgasm thieves.

I hope.

This is one hell of a jewel heist, I think to myself as I look at Dec's package.

"Where?" I mouth.

He points to the bathroom.

I shake my head.

He points downstairs.

I nod.

Nonverbal communication is ingrained in us these days, a necessity for living in a home with a baby whose precious sleep cycles represent our freedom. Yes, we have a nanny. Yes, Mom and Dad have her three days a week. But I don't want to be away from Ellie as much as I am.

That surprised me when I went back to work.

Surprised me more than I want to admit.

So Dec and I are in perpetual disagreement over how much time Ellie spends being cared for by anyone other than Mom and Dad. It's not that Mia, our part-time nanny, isn't fabulous. Declan found her through an agency that places native-speaking Mandarin Chinese nannies in homes with families who want their children exposed to the language early, for bilinguality.

Go ahead. Roll your eyes. I did, too.

Until Mia came.

As we make our way through the living room, the glow of the Christmas tree making me smile, I realize all our nonverbal skills are part of a larger constellation of blessings.

I'm married to a wonderful man.

He's an outstanding father.

We have plenty of money.

My parents are loving.

Our daughter is healthy and sweet, her nanny is fabulous and trustworthy.

Tears fill my eyes as we pause in the living room. Dec eyes the couch.

My nonverbal *no* is loud and clear.

Outside, the moon lights up the backyard, where it looks like the Waterford Crystal factory exploded. I knew the weather forecast said there might be ice, but nothing like this. My eyes dart to the stove clock, the orange numbers bright and clear. 2:52 a.m.

Power's still on.

Pressing his hands against the thick glass sliders, Declan peers outside, then turns to me, hand extended. I snuggle up to him, the cold glass making me shiver.

"What about that?" he asks, pointing.

"What?"

"Out there."

"You want to have sex outside?"

"Not outside. The shed."

"You want to have a quickie in Dad's man cave?"

"It's looking like our best alternative."

"No way. I refuse to have sex next to my father's pee can."

"His what?"

"No."

He sighs. We reach the kitchen, where Declan is examining Chuffy's doggie bed with a little too much interest. I kick his ankle.

He yelps.

That innocent, playful little kick sets off a chain reaction. Chuffy scrambles up and starts growling, his space invaded by two people who don't live here, one doing a very good imitation of a chubby candy cane.

(Hint: That would be me.)

The other one looks like he has a green-and-white-striped candy cane in his pants.

(Hint: That would be Declan.)

"*Woof! Woof!*" the white puffball growls, protecting Jason and Marie Jacoby's house from these horrible, sex-crazed invaders who just want to steal an orgasm or two from each other.

Chuffy's barks trigger Chuckles, who slinks into the room like a lion prowling the savanna, senses up and ready for battle.

Until Dec, moving backwards, accidentally steps on his tail.

There must be muscles on a cat's body that do not behave according to any known measure of kinesiology, because somehow, with his tail beneath Declan's bare sole, Chuckles jumps up, front claws splayed, and climbs Declan's thighs, stopping just at his crotch, pure fury on our cat's face.

A silent scream freezes my poor husband's face in agony.

And this, ladies and gentlemen, is the part where I must confess that my reaction was subpar.

Because I start laughing.

Hysterically.

"Need. Help." Declan's grunts shake me out of it. I gingerly reach for Chuckles just as Chuffy comes over, puts his paws on Declan's shin, and starts licking Chuckles' butthole.

I've never seen a cat move so fast.

Up poor Declan's body.

"*Woof! Woof!*" Chuffy barks, then makes chase for Chuckles.

Declan is folded in half like a Christmas card.

"Help," he says, voice low and tortured.

"What can I do?"

Standing straight, he pulls his pajama pants down, unveiling an impressive... yule log.

"Seriously, Dec? Now? Here? After that?"

"I'm examining the damage, Shannon. Not inviting you to take a joyride."

"Oh." I drop down and look, squinting. Red holes

"Last time I had a puncture wound there, it was from the EpiPen you jabbed in me."

"Chuckles didn't do it on purpose, and neither did I. Is your penith—uh, *penis*—okay?"

"No penis is okay after that, Shannon. And my penis is never just 'okay.' Don't use that word to describe it."

"What word should I use?"

He opens his mouth to tell me, when suddenly, Tyler appears.

"*Santa?*"

Oh, no. My heart sinks.

Childhood magic is sacred in our family. One of the few ways you could disappoint my mom or dad would be to take away the magic of fantasy from a kid. They delayed and delayed and *delayed* the truth about Santa, the Easter Bunny, the Tooth Fairy.

Tyler is eight, so definitely on the older side of believing, especially in this day and age of the internet, where you can look up *anything*.

Jeffrey has figured that one out, much to Carol's chagrin.

Tyler hasn't.

Fortunately, Declan's turned away, and his pants aren't down in the back, so it's easy to fix his flagrante delicto status without Tyler seeing anything.

Fixing the confusion in his eyes as he realizes we're not Santa isn't so easy.

"Where's Santa?"

Nervously, I look in the living room, where "Santa" set everything up last night after we made the kids go to bed. "He's, well..."

Declan rescues me. "*Shhhh*, Tyler, buddy." Hands on his shoulders, he moves Tyler around the back way to the stairs. "Santa can only come to houses where the kids are asleep."

"Can't sleep." Panic floods his face. When Tyler is anxious, he loses some of his language ability. Apraxia is such a strange condition, shrouded in so much mystery. Unpredictable communication is the least of it. But we know one thing: panic makes it worse.

"It's okay."

"Can't sleep! Santa won't come!" Tears, loud and raw, begin in earnest.

I realize instantly what's happening and take him from Declan. I bend down and hug him first. Comforting him is more important that getting him to understand, because he can't understand words when he's panicked.

"*Shhhh. Shhhh.* Santa is coming. No matter what, honey."

"Want Santa to come!"

I look him in the eye, the final traces of little-boyhood fading so fast. Red, tear-filled eyes look back at me, serious and desperate. "Santa will come even if you pretend to sleep."

"Pretend?"

"Do you understand pretend?"

"Not real."

"Yes. Not real. So if you go to bed and close your eyes, you can pretend to sleep. Then Santa will come."

"You will pretend to sleep and Santa will come." That's another part of apraxia: Tyler confuses pronouns when he gets stressed out.

"That's right."

A shadow behind Tyler makes me look up. It's Carol, giving me a wide-eyed nonverbal look that asks, *What's going on?*

"Look, Tyler." He turns around and gives Carol a

worried look, like he's done something wrong and is afraid of getting in trouble.

She opens her arms. He walks into the hug.

"Santa will come. You will pretend to sleep," he mutters into her arm.

"Okay," she says uncertainly, looking at me for direction. I just shrug.

He looks up at her. "You need to pee."

Declan snickers, his hand on his thigh where Chuckles nailed him.

Carol just shakes her head with a smile. "Let's get you to the bathroom, then bed, Tyler."

"Then Santa will come. Only pretend to sleep."

Sharp mom's eyes meet mine. "You told him that?"

"*You* told *me* that when we were kids!"

A throaty laugh that sounds just like our mother comes out of her. "I guess I did. It worked, right? Kept you in bed."

"Parenting is all about the bottom line. Whatever works."

She looks at my hand, holding the baby monitor for Ellie. "Guess so. What are you two doing downstairs?"

My imitation of a speechless fish gives it away. Dec clears his throat and looks down at his crotch, tenderly touching the puncture wounds under his pajamas pants, unaware of, um, how this looks.

"Seriously?" she hisses. "You two can't hold back for one night?"

"That's not–this isn't–it's–"

"Goodnight. I'm putting Tyler to bed. And if you need a quickie, do what all the other parents of little kids on the planet do–have se–," she halts, looking at Tyler, "I mean, *wrap presents* in the bathroom. Why do you think bathroom carpets are so plush?"

Even Tyler gives her the stink eye over *that*.

"I—we—"

"And for God's sake, lock the door!"

With that, she and Tyler disappear.

A warm, friendly arm goes around my shoulders, fingertips going for my breast. "She's got a point."

I look down at his crotch. "So do you, now."

"The bathroom's not all that bad—"

Static crackles suddenly from the baby monitor in my hand. "MUH MUH NUH NUH!"

I make a beeline for the stairs, Dec behind me.

"So much for a little Christmas nookie," he hisses. "Chuckles got closer to having sex with me than you did."

"Ewwww! Don't joke about having sex with Chuckles!"

"You need to rub some antibiotic cream on those puncture wounds," I tell him.

"That's not the kind of rubbing I was aiming for tonight," he grunts, ignoring my advice.

We walk into the room to find Ellie standing up in her crib, hands on the railing.

She looks at me, then Declan, and says,

"DA DA UMBUH!"

He plops down on the bed, hands behind his head on the pillow as he stares at the ceiling like it's Chuckles. "See?" he mutters, turning on his side as I settle her to the breast. "Genius. The kid is a genius."

And then he pretends to sleep.

Maybe it will help Santa come tonight.

But sadly, poor Declan won't.

CHAPTER 11

"Snap, crackle, pop!" Dad says as I wander into the kitchen at the buttcrack of dawn, Ellie on my hip. Following his eyes, I look outside at the glittering ice palace of the yard.

"Wow," I whisper, shuffling to the counter like a zombie.

"Guh guh guh," she says to him, grinning.

"Someone's an early bird!" he says to her.

"Didn't inherit it from me." Unaccustomed to a drip coffeemaker, my mind blanks for a second. As I remember, I grab the handle of the carafe and pour the coffee into my mug. "What happened to the espresso machine we gave you guys?" I ask.

"Amy claimed it."

"*What?*"

"Also, honey," he says sheepishly. "We like the coffee this machine makes better than what you guys have."

I look at him in mock horror. "Don't tell Declan that! It's like telling Mom you like Miracle Whip better than mayo!"

"*Shhhhh!* She hasn't figured it out yet."

I find some milk, splash it into the sad excuse for caffeine water, and start drinking. If I consume three cups of this, it equals one shot of espresso.

I think. Maybe.

I don't know. Math-ing this early is hard.

"Tyler and Jeffrey are still asleep?" I ask, looking at the clock. Five forty-two.

"I told them they couldn't get up until six."

"Better than three a.m. Tyler woke up then."

"He did? Did he see that Santa came?"

"No."

"What did he see?"

I blush and stammer, "Nothing." The image of Declan's fiasco with Chuckles and Chuffy floods my memory banks.

Dad scoops Ellie out of my arms, settles her into the high chair, and sprinkles Cheerios on her tray. She gobbles them up like caviar as Dad disappears down the dark hallway.

"Hey," Declan says, appearing like a catalog model for Hanna Andersson. Mussed hair and a slight five-o'clock shadow make him sexy. Casual. Homey and comfortable.

Except it's not supposed to be a five a.m. shadow...

I point to the coffee maker. He looks.

The most astonished expression crosses his face. "What is *that?*" He points, finger extended like Ellie, the gesture childlike. Gawking. Utterly consumed by novelty.

"A Mr. Coffee machine."

"I haven't seen one of those since the faculty lounge in high school."

"Welcome to my parents' house."

"It's the coffee equivalent of a buggy whip."

"I know."

"What happened to the machine we gave them?"

"Amy took it for her apartment."

"We could have given her one of her own!"

"I know. Mom and Dad like their drip machine."

"Do they also snack on cyanide and enjoy being flayed as a hobby?"

I'm about to answer him when the human equivalent of an air-raid siren appears.

"SAAAAAAAAAAAAAANNNNNTTTTTT-TAAAAAA CAAAAAAAAAMMMMMEEEEE!" screams Tyler as the predictable *thump thump thump* of little feet comes down the staircase, his face so excited, it's infectious.

Ellie starts clapping, a Cheerio stuck to her lower lip.

Declan grabs my coffee and sniffs. His face goes sour.

"Daddy Humbug," I whisper as I grab my coffee and chug it.

"Daddy's even more humbug now. No sex *and* bad coffee," Declan whispers back, one eye on my dad. "They say hell is other people, but I'm pretty sure it's *this*."

"HHHHEEEELLLLLOOOOOOO!" Mom squeals from around the corner.

"It's like God said, 'Hold my beer,'" Declan mutters as Carol comes into the kitchen, pours the last of the coffee, and grins at us.

"You two get in a little holiday cheer last night?" *Wink.*

Mom is in her glory. "I want everyone by the tree! We need to take our first-thing-in-the-morning Christmas picture! I want it to look natural!"

I peer at her. "You're wearing fake eyelashes."

"What? I am not!"

"Mom, you have more makeup on than a fifteen-year-old YouTube vlogger. I could take a credit card to your face, scrape an inch, and use it to paint five Bob Ross paintings."

"I don't know what you are talking about." She pulls her hair off her shoulder, her fingernails a perfect pattern of red, white, and green. Are those silver bells in the center of each nail?

"Come on, Mom. You look like Dad took out the compressor and sprayed all your makeup on."

"What? No! I woke up like this!" She squares her shoulders, flips her hair back, and does her best Morgan-Fairchild-on-*The-Love-Boat* imitation.

"After falling into a vat of concealer?"

"PICTURE TIME!" she shouts. People start to migrate in front of the tree, a big, fat Fraser Fir from Nova Scotia that looks like Dad must have built the house around it. He had to trim a foot off the bottom to make it fit in the room with the star on it.

We all groan in unison as Amy appears in the doorway, long, red, curly hair a tangled mess in front of her face. "Coffee?" she mutters as Mom storms over and pulls her into the living room.

"Look at my girls!" Mom gushes as we line up like the von Trapp children in *The Sound of Music*. "You are adorable!"

Chuffy waddles in, tail wagging, the bane of Chuckles' existence.

Or maybe that's Mom, because Chuckles comes into the room next... dressed just like Dad, Declan, Jeffrey, and Tyler.

"MOM! You made Chuckles wear green-and-white-striped pajamas?" Carol moans, horrified.

"Of course! He's a boy!"

"Grandma!" Jeffrey calls out, his voice turning to the

familiar lecture tone he's recently adopted. "I told you that's not fair."

"Why is Chuffy in red-and-white-striped pajamas? When did Chuffy become a girl?" Dad asks.

Mom's mouth goes tight. Or, at least, it tries to. Has she started using Botox? "The website where I ordered the family pajamas was out of boy dog outfits, so Chuffy is an honorary girl this year. Won't make that mistake again. I need to shop earlier."

"When did you order?" Dad asks her.

"July."

"No, Grandma. Chuffy isn't a girl. They are an enby."

"What's an enby?"

"N.B.," Jeffrey explains. "Enby is how you say NB, and NB stands for nonbinary."

"What does that mean?"

"It means sometimes Chuffy is a girl and sometimes Chuffy is a boy."

"But, honey," Carol says in that voice parents develop for trying to say the right thing on the fly, "We can't know Chuffy's gender identity. The outfit Grandma got is only wrong because she has an overdeveloped need for the surface level to be perfect."

"That's right!" Mom crows, as if that's a compliment. "So let's get perfection going." She claps twice. "NOW!"

"I haven't even had coffee!" Amy groans, looking like an extra in a zombie movie. A candy-cane zombie.

"You can get caffeine after we smile for the camera!"

"How can I smile when I don't have caffeine, Mom?"

"Fake it like everyone else, sweetie!"

Dad gets the long selfie stick and we cram in like fans at a ComiCon in a photobooth with Felicia Day.

"Say cheese!" Mom calls out.

No one does.

"Everyone wave and say 'Merry Christmas!'"

Everyone does except Declan, who grunts, "Bad coffee."

Click.

"Ellie! Look what Santa brought you! Come on, Jason! I'm making a video!" Mom flits across the living room.

"Make sure your thumb isn't over the lens!" Dad warns her. "Like last year."

"Santa's here!" she shouts. The caffeine-deprived half of us groan, while the rest of us watch the kids.

"I got a robot! Santa brought me the robot kit! I got the robot kit!" Tyler screams. Every adult eye in the room catches another, the group effort to get Tyler his incredibly expensive—by family standards—gift worth it, just from the look on his face. Declan and I have learned not to give anything too big as a gift, instead diverting money for Jeffrey and Tyler into college savings accounts. We sat Carol down a long time ago and explained that by the time the boys are eighteen, they'll be fully funded for wherever they want to go.

It's the least we could do.

We contribute our share to group efforts like this, because it's more fun for everyone to be an equal part of it. Especially seeing the look on my little nephew's face.

"Want to open it now!" he crows, examining the box that says, "1,572 pieces of fun!"

Dad's turn to groan. "Let's open it later, when I have my tools and my glasses, and we have some space."

"And when I'm wearing shoes," Carol adds. "I've managed the LEGO Barefoot Parent Challenge just fine, but metal robot pieces? I need to up my game."

"It's only 5:59!" Amy calls out. "We weren't allowed to

get up until 6:30 when we were kids!" Her voice has that tone of The Youngest in the Family, an accusing whine of entitlement and perceived betrayal.

We just call it Amy's voice.

"We've softened," Dad informs her, moving to the kitchen to grab a metal can of ground supermarket coffee, using a big scoop to measure it in the basket filter. Declan watches Dad's movements like he's being forced to observe waterboarding as a hostage.

"Declan! Shannon!" Mom calls out. "Come see Ellie's present from Santa!"

Given that we know exactly what she got, this is just for show, but we humor her, coming into the living room and–

"WHAT IS *THAT*?" I shout.

Ellie is playing with a puppy. A *live* puppy.

"Ellie wuvs her widdle Wuffy!" Mom says in a syrupy baby voice. She holds the puppy in front of Ellie, who is sitting in the middle of the room, surrounded by all of us (minus Dad). Jeffrey is opening his gaming system, Tyler is reading the box of his robot toy. The stockings are still on the mantel, untouched but not for long.

I take all of that in via peripheral vision, because I'm entirely focused on my mother and my baby, who is burying her fingers in the white puff of dog fur Mom holds before her, the puppy's pink tongue turning Ellie's cheek into a salt lick.

"Wuffy?" Jeffrey asks, not taking his eyes off his Santa score.

"That's just a placeholder name. Ellie can pick the name later!" Mom chirps.

"Santa did *not* bring Ellie a puppy!" I shout, Dec at my side in an instant, giving Mom the highest cocked eyebrow ever. Pretty sure it touches the moon.

"He didn't?" she says with a high, nervous laugh, testing me out.

"No, Mom. He did *not*." Dec is there as backup, if I need him, but for now, he lets me tackle this one.

Mom backpedals so hard, it's like she's doing the Tour de France backwards.

"What? No! Of course not! Santa brought *me* the puppy." Mom's shifty eyes look over at Dad, whose eyebrow looks like Declan's twin.

This smells like a cover story.

"Good. I'm glad Santa brought *you* a new puppy, Mom," I say, moving Ellie to the ride-on toy Santa *actually* brought her. "Because we're not taking a puppy home. We already have Chuckles."

"Chuckles is boring."

Dec touches his thigh. "Literally. Those claws bore in deep."

Mom gives him a funny look.

Dec gives it right back.

"I thought Santa only brought gifts for little kids, Grandma," Jeffrey challenges Mom. "Where are Santa's presents for all the other adults if he brought one for you?"

I can't believe my mother thought she could pass off a live puppy as a gift for a baby.

Oh. Wait. It's my mother.

I *can* believe it.

Emergency sirens begin in the distance, growing louder as they get close, saving Mom from having to answer Jeffrey's question. We all stop as the red flashing lights go past, the ambulance slow and steady.

"Oh, no! Poor saps," Dad says as he rejoins us, the coffee maker gurgling behind him. "On Christmas morning, no less. I wonder where they're going."

"Maybe it's because of all the ice," Jeffrey muses as he grabs his stocking from the mantel and starts fishing around for the candy he knows is in there.

"Oh, no, you don't!" Mom catches him. "Not yet."

"But all you're doing is talking!"

"No sugar highs until after breakfast."

"SIX!" Amy shouts. "It's finally six a.m. How can I be up at six a.m. and not have coffee?"

Dad interrupts the drip drip drip, pouring her a cup, the coffee drops hissing on the open burner before he can replace the carafe. "Here." A long, steady stream of pent-up brew flows into the carafe as the burnt scent of drippage fills the room.

"It's like watching someone wash their car with holy water," Declan grouses.

"Or using anointed oil as lube," I say in agreement.

"Please don't bring up sex," he says in a tight voice.

"Sorry."

"Not half as sorry as I am." The frown on his face matches Chuckles, who snuggles up to the fireplace and closes his eyes, chubby body encased in stripes that make him look like a Brach's peppermint.

"Oh, WOW!" Jeffrey shouts from the front window. "It looks like Elsa came!"

"Who is Elsa?" Dec asks me.

"From *Frozen*?"

Blank look.

"The Disney movie?"

Blank look.

"'Let It Go'?"

"I'm trying, Shannon, but when I get excited because I think there's a chance, and then the cat punctures my crotch, it's a little hard to let it go."

"No, no, Dec, I'm talking about the song from the movie *Frozen*. 'Let It Go'?"

He shrugs.

"If Ellie were born five years ago, you'd have that song memorized," Carol says. "I wonder what movie your kid will latch onto. My life has been nothing but *The Lego Movie* and *Transformers* for the last decade or so."

"I like *Frozen*, too!" Jeffrey argues.

And then he starts singing the song.

Bewildered, Declan stares at our nephew like he's a circus act. Jeffrey, enjoying the attention, belts out the entire song, including the key change and octave shift. The kid isn't going to hit those high notes next year.

Better "enjoy" them while we can.

Ellie claps for him when he's done.

"YA YA!" she cries out, then finds a piece of fuzz on the carpet that is worthy of her focus.

The sound of bacon sizzling in the kitchen breaks through the chatter. Three seconds later, the scent wafts in.

"*Mmmm*, bacon," Mom shouts, sidestepping her grandson, who turns to me with a look that is *soooooo* Jacoby.

"She thinks she can distract me, but that only works on little kids, Auntie Shannon."

"*Mmmm*, bacon," Declan says to me, turning away.

Bacon apparently works on thirty-something-year-old men, too.

Dad sits down in front of the fireplace and starts assembling a fire, setting the wood in a perfect stack, a combination of space for airflow, kindling, crumpled newspaper, and the just-right ratio of thick-to-thin logs. I don't know how he does it, but he always manages to get the fires just right, so that in a few hours, the perfect coals for roasting marshmallows will make us beg for sticks and the ever-present bag of white puffy goodness.

Then again, it's Christmas. Once the pies and fudge come out, we're probably going to abandon the marsh–

Oh, who am I kidding? I'll just pull out my holiday-dinner yoga pants and eat whatever I want.

In the kitchen, Chef Dad has two separate Belgian-waffle makers ready to deploy. Once he finishes getting the fire going, he starts cracking eggs into a big bowl to scramble, and has an oiled-up electric griddle in front of him. The sizzling bacon on the stove is just a start, another few pounds on trays in the oven, slow cooking. Jason Jacoby may not have jets and mansions and wealth, but he's the best Christmas-morning short-order cook you could ever ask for.

"PROTEIN!" Carol shouts at her kids from the living room. "PROTEIN FIRST!"

I glare at Dec, because I know a nasty joke about his personal protein factory is about to come my way.

No, uh, pun intended.

Oh, geez. Even when I try to avoid a porny joke from my husband, *I* end up making one.

"First batch of waffles are up!" Dad shouts. "Plain!" As the morning goes on, he'll make some with blueberries in them. Chocolate chips. On the counter, there are jars of peanut butter and Nutella. The butter was left out last night so it's nice and soft. A big glass jug of maple syrup from a local sugar shack is front and center in the lineup.

"Life is good," Declan murmurs as he fills his plate. I give him a nudge.

"See? It's not all bad."

"PRESENTS!" Tyler shouts. "Want to open presents!"

"After we eat," Carol says, already weary. "Every year we tell you the same thing. Why do you keep pushing?"

"Because maybe one year you'll say yes," Jeffrey answers. Dec has just shoved a big piece of maple-syrup-covered waffle in his mouth. He eyes Jeffrey. I know that look.

Dec thinks Jeffrey is a shark.

And admires him.

"I never say yes," his mom snaps back.

"Not yet."

Dad appears with another Belgian waffle, plunking it on the serving plate. Jeffrey snatches it up, takes a bite while staring straight into Carol's eyes, and starts chewing.

"God help me when you're a teen."

Jeffrey gives her a half-chewed-waffle grin.

We work our way through the smorgasbord of food options, Declan miserably trying to get some caffeine in him, me working on teaching Ellie to try a blueberry (nope!) and drink a little orange juice from her sippy cup (success!).

A fire truck goes by, lights flashing, sirens off.

"What's going on?" Dad asks, walking to the radio, flipping it on.

"Jason! Really? The radio?"

"I'm worried, Marie." WBZ AM radio comes on, the announcer's voice unchanged since my childhood (or at least, it seems like it).

"*—ice storm of unprecedented thickness has shut down interstates and backroads throughout much of Massachusetts, Connecticut, and Rhode Island. We turn to—*"

"What?" Gasps from our group block out the announcer. Dad shushes us.

"*—more than 80,000 Massachusetts residents are without power.*"

Temperatures are expected to rise sharply through the morning and afternoon, leading to an unusually quick thaw, Jim. The weight of the melting ice could snap more branches and bring down power lines. Crews are being dispatched from five states, forcing line workers to leave Christmas morning celebrations and—"

Mom looks around the house. "But *we* have power!"

"—the towns of Grafton, Upton, Mendon, Milford, and Hopkinton were hit hardest in a strange oval that brought sleet and freezing rain and took out—"

"That's us!" Jeffrey squeals. "*We're* Mendon!"

"*SHHHHHH!*" we all hush him.

"—93 percent of households without power in Grafton, 91 percent in Upton, 96 percent in Mendon, and—"

"We got lucky," I whisper to Declan.

"Power could still go out if a fast thaw makes tree branches too heavy and bogged down," he points out.

Just then, Mom's phone rings. Reflexively, Declan pats his chest, where his phone would be if he were wearing a suit jacket.

"Where's my phone?" Mom asks, setting off the hunt. By the time we figure out which one is hers, the ringing stops. She checks the number.

"Agnes DuChamp?" Her eyes cut over to Dad. "Why would Agnes call me on Christmas?"

"Aren't you two friends?" Declan asks.

"No. She's a fine woman, but no. She's my student, not my buddy."

"You invited her to a sex toy party," Carol notes.

"And our wedding, and my baby shower," I point out.

"That doesn't make her a call-you-on-Christmas-morning friend!" Mom protests.

"Maybe she needs help, Marie," Dad says, concern permeating his voice. The atmosphere in the house changes, Carol going to the thermostat and turning it up, Dad moving to look at the phone over Mom's shoulder. In New England, a massive ice storm like this means you take precautions, and never, ever assume that having power *now* means you'll have power *later*.

"Seventy-four okay?" Carol calls out from the hall. If we increase the house temperature before the electricity goes and the furnace can't run, we can help prevent pipes from freezing.

"Sure," Dad calls back. "Jeffrey, can you go get about twelve more big pieces of firewood from the breezeway?" Without complaint, Jeffrey does as asked, Tyler at his heels.

"Where are the sleeping bags?" Dad asks Amy. "Let's pull them out, just in case."

"Why would you need those?" Declan asks.

"In case the power really goes out and we need to hunker down."

"Surely we can just leave if that—"

Three different phones start ringing.

Dad's isn't one of them. Carol, Mom, and Amy all answer. Dad stands in the small foyer by the front door, putting on boots and a coat. He opens the narrow coat-closet door and roots around for something, emerging with what look like tiny BDSM torture devices with little grippies on the end of spider-like rubber webs.

Which he attaches to the soles of his shoes.

"I'm heading around the neighborhood to see what's up. Shannon, can you marshal the crew to do breakfast clean up? I'll be right back."

The door shuts just as Mom approaches, brow down with worry.

"That was Agnes's granddaughter, Cassie. She said Agnes lost power in the middle of the night, and has

121

medications that need to be kept at an even temperature. And something about a medical device that requires electricity. I told her to bring Agnes over right away."

"Mom?" Carol pokes her head in. "You know my co-worker, Josh? He might need to come over later. He's visiting his new boyfriend's family in Grafton and they don't have power."

"Oh, dear," Mom says, eyes darting everywhere, contemplating. "This is quite a situation! Where's Jason?"

"He went outside to check out the neighborhood," I say in the most soothing voice I can muster, hoping to take the edge off her worry.

No such luck.

"I need to talk to Dave," Dec says to me. "Who knows what this is doing to HQ. And I'm cold."

"Carol just turned the heat up."

He looks down at his pajamas. "Still cold."

"You're just looking for an excuse to change."

"Don't need an excuse."

"Take Ellie with you?" I hand her off to him.

"Why? Does she hate these pajamas as much as I do?"

"No, silly. But she could use a diaper change, and I need to deal with this."

"This?"

I jerk my head toward Mom. "*This*. Her. Mom. You want to trade jobs?"

He walks upstairs holding Ellie.

Just then, Dad comes back in, the sun beaming off the ice everywhere. It's blinding. We all gasp as the door opens. He shakes his head.

"It's a mess. Looks like our block is the only one with power. Hard to tell because it's daylight, but there's a straight line to the main road. Everyone from the Turners to the south and the Essalis to the north has power, but the other houses look like they don't."

"We're in the four percent!" Jeffrey calls out. "That's cool!"

A loud crack outside, then a crazy, glasslike crash, make us look behind Dad. A branch the diameter of Jeffrey's arm and about twelve feet long has snapped off the small tree to the right, and fallen, a greenstick fracture that leaves the exposed wood looking like drunken toothpicks in a container.

"Jason!" Mom shouts, alarmed eyes connecting with Dad, emotions overflowing. "You were just there!" Mom's panicked voice makes my heart race.

"I'm fine, Marie." He points to the branch. "That's the major problem," Dad says. "We have no idea when a branch might knock out *our* power."

"Better get more wood!" Carol calls out as Mom looks at the tree and frowns.

"We need to open presents!" Mom argues.

"This is more important, Grandma," Jeffrey says seriously. "We need to make sure we have provisions and heat before we think about luxuries like presents."

"Where did you *come* from?" Carol asks, gawking. "It's like someone transplanted a prepper's baby into my womb."

Jeffrey grins at her before heading to the breezeway.

"His father's idea of being prepared was to make sure he never ran out of vodka," she mutters to me. "And a power outage meant he couldn't watch porn."

I look quickly for Ellie. *Whew.*

"Please don't say that word."

"What word? Vodka?"

"Porn."

123

"Why?"

"Ellie will repeat it if she hears it."

"And you know this... how?"

"Don't ask."

Genuine concern washes over her face. "Is Declan... are you two having marriage problems?"

"What? God, no!"

"I mean, I found you two downstairs trying to have sex in the middle of the night. Does he have some kind of sex addiction?"

"Carol."

Wide eyes meet mine, the edges filled with a teasing mirth that reminds me of a craftier version of Mom. "What? I'm just worried about you. Besides, no guy can be as perfect as Declan. He has to have a flaw."

"Being a sex addict is a flaw?"

"It's more like a feature. Not a bug."

"Shut up, Carol."

Laughter is all I get in response as she walks away.

"Did I just hear you say that Declan is a sex fiend?" Mom asks as she passes Carol, who laughs even louder.

"What?"

"Lucky dog."

Speaking of dogs, the puppy wriggles over to us, squats, and pees all over Mom's cream-colored rug.

Ding dong! The doorbell cuts in as Mom frets over the puppy's accident, Jeffrey and Tyler start circling the wrapped presents under the tree like hipsters in line for the new iPhone, and suddenly, I'm standing alone in the doorway to the kitchen, holding someone else's cup of lukewarm coffee.

Christmas morning just got very, very nontraditional.

I look into the circle of the coffee mug. Nothing I do

will change the ice storm, but I can improve one situation: my caffeine intake. When you're the one who makes the coffee, you get to calibrate the strength. I find the basket filters, open the can of coffee and triple the amount Dad uses.

Water and a switch-flip later and the coffee is brewing. With bad coffee, no amount of concentration will ever make it taste good, but if I view it purely as a supply of bloodstream caffeine, utilitarianism makes it palatable.

Man, have I come a long way since I met Declan, when my kitchen cupboards were full of free instant-coffee samples from various chains I mystery shopped and my idea of really exotic coffee was gourmet hazelnut.

Or anything with froth.

"Marie, I told you we needed puppy pads!" Dad calls out from the living room.

"I wrapped some! They're under the tree, with Ellie's name on them."

"So you *did* plan to give my daughter a live puppy?" I call back from the kitchen as I pour a cup from the still-brewing machine.

"Of course, Shannon! It's not like I'd give her a dead puppy. No one is that cruel!"

"That's not the point!" I fume, coming into the living room to find Dad on his knees, blotting the puppy's mess, and Mom holding a long match, lit.

"Being cruel to puppies most certainly *is* the point! How can you accuse me of killing a puppy and gifting it to a baby!"

"That's not—we're not talking about—" I sputter.

Dec appears with my happy baby and normal clothes on his tense body. He starts humming the song "Let It Go."

I offer him my cup of coffee. "Here. I made you some."

Tentative, he takes a sip, mouth puckering. "What is this?"

"Hell."

"Coffee hell is more watered down than this."

"I didn't say coffee hell. Just hell."

"What's wrong?"

"My mother."

"Say no more."

The *shuffle clunk, shuffle clunk* of something big moving one step at a time invades my hearing. Agnes appears, the feet of her walker covered with split, bright-red tennis balls, festive Christmas lights twisted around the contraption. There's a bumper sticker on the front, wrapped around the frame, that reads, "I Brake for Naked Hitchhikers."

Huh. Wonder what *that's* about?

"Hello!" says a woman's cheery, high-pitched voice. "Merry Christmas!" That would be Corrine Morris, Agnes' best friend. The two old ladies are a hoot, but they are also wildly inappropriate.

Which means Amanda and I always watch them closely for clues on how to be a badass old lady.

Declan sets Ellie down and we watch her snowflake butt crawl off towards the couch, smiling together. Dec takes my elbow and starts to steer me to the hallway. "Shannon, I want to get you alone."

"Sex? You want sex now?"

"No, no. Not sex. Can we talk?"

Mom is chattering away in the other room, helping Agnes with her medical machinery and medications, while Corrine pets Chuffy and enjoys the roaring fire. It's a picture of neighborly and family goodness, one I want to take in and let infuse me.

Declan's eyes are warm and loving, his tension at bay, the early-morning hijinks a world I love.

"Of course," I tell him. "Why don't we go over here and—"

"We're all gonna die! The world is ending!" Jeffrey screams, interrupting me suddenly, the freak-out coming out of nowhere.

"What? Why do you think that?" Carol asks, clearly flummoxed, like the rest of us.

"Because Grandma actually *lit* the fancy Christmas candles! I'm twelve and I've never seen them lit! She always says hell will freeze over before she does that!"

Tyler looks outside. "Ice is everywhere. Hell is frozen."

Both boys start to make loud sounds of distress.

Declan starts humming "The Imperial Death March."

My dad's disembodied head appears around the corner between the kitchen and the dining room. "Did you say Marie *lit* those candles?"

Jeffrey looks at Dad with the exact same expression of horror. "YES!"

Dad blinks rapidly, then suddenly, like thundersnow, bellows, "MARIE! WHAT IS GOING ON?"

Agnes picks that exact moment to walk by, her walker moving inch by inch. Her neck turns and her eyebrows shoot up to the chandelier above the table. "Marie lit the decorative candles? You got a bomb shelter somewhere, Jason? Because she knows something we don't."

Jeffrey starts crying. Carol moves to him, putting her arm around his shoulders. "Sweetie, what's wrong?"

He points at Agnes. "She's old. She's wise. When the wise people start worrying, it's bad."

"Just because she's old doesn't mean she's wise," Corrine cracks as she scoots past Agnes, using only a cane.

"Shut up, Corrine. You wouldn't know a wise person if their dentures bit you on the ass."

"At least I have an ass, Agnes. Yours looks like a pancake got into a fight with a Zamboni."

Great. Now I'm staring at Agnes's ass.

It's definitely the apocalypse.

"I lit them because I realized I don't want to be one of those old ladies who dies and her kids find all the good china they never saw before and unused beautiful table-cloths folded up in the closet. I want to enjoy life while I'm still here," Mom says in a defensive tone.

Agnes squints at the mantel. "That's an awfully thick taper candle."

"It's fine." Mom sticks her nose close. "It smells so nice. Cinnamon. Ahhhhhh." Her mouth is open as she over-plays it.

"Does that red taper candle have *veins*?" Corrine asks, walking swiftly, barely using her cane. Before she reaches the mantel, she gasps. "Marie! That's the penis candle from June Mantini's granddaughter's bridal shower!"

"WHAT?" Mom blows it out, grabs it, and looks around furtively as she tosses it into the lit fire in the fire-place. "Oops!"

Declan curls his palm around the corner of his mouth and turns away, pulling me close to whisper, "I can't watch."

The candle makes a strange hissing sound as it melts, going from a solid ten inches to an unimpressive lump of soft tissue.

Mom turns on the television and points the remote at the 55" LED screen. Last year, Dad grudgingly let Declan and me give them the new TV. Hauling out the old Sylvania Dad got at a Black Friday sale in 2001 was like being a pallbearer at an old teacher's funeral.

"NECN says the whole region's been wiped out. Just pockets of electricity in select towns," Mom gasps, reading the closed-captioning as if the rest of us aren't literate.

"Confirms what WBZ said," Dad says with a sigh.

"We *really* got lucky!" I whisper.

"We sure did," Declan says under his breath, squeezing my ample ass. "No Zambonis or pancakes here."

I swat him.

He pinches me. "What are the chances of getting out to your dad's man cave alone?"

I look around the crowded room. "About zero."

"But you didn't say *absolute* zero. *About* means there's a chance."

"Says the master negotiator."

Ding dong!

Carol answers the door. It's Josh.

"Here we go," Declan mutters.

"I guess it'll just be a bigger holiday."

"No. I mean it. Here, we *go*. Time to go."

"You want to leave?"

"Yes."

"Now?"

"Ideally, ten minutes ago, but now will do."

"DECLAN!" I shout.

The entire house goes quiet. All you can hear is a melting penis candle and the crackle of ice falling outside. I don't yell at Declan in public. *Ever*. We're known as the couple who never, ever raise their voices. Never call each other names.

So I'm putting on an unexpected show.

"May we speak in private?" he asks tersely, the question more of a command.

"You want to leave *now*?" I reply.

Mom starts making hitched breathing sounds like she's either choking on another penis candle or Lush is having an eighty-percent-off sale.

"It's me, isn't it?" Josh whisper-screams. "I show up and you don't want to be around me. I knew my body odor was bad, but not *that* bad!"

Carol pats his arm. "No, it's pretty bad, actually."

"You really can't help yourself, can you?" he snaps.

"IT WAS THE PENIS CANDLE, WASN'T IT?" Mom sobs. "You saw me burn it. You think I'm a pervert!"

"That's not why people think you're a pervert, Marie," Josh replies.

"Oooo, snap!" Carol offers him a fistbump. He snarls at her.

"I'm still salty from that BO comment."

"You'll thaw if I compliment your new belt."

He brightens. "I will! Isn't it gorgeous? Mom gave it to me."

"Shannon?" Declan says, pulling me away from them. "We need to talk."

"Not if you want to leave."

"I think it's getting chaotic and Ellie's having a hard time emotionally."

Peals of laughter come from our baby. She's on the floor, surrounded by Amy, Tyler, and Jeffrey as they roll a ball to each other, the new puppy following it with the energy of a hummingbird.

"Yes, she's clearly distraught," I deadpan.

"Fine. *I* want to leave."

"Why?"

"Because this isn't a family gathering anymore. It's a Red Cross shelter," he whispers. He holds up his iPhone. "And my phone battery is close to dead. I left my charger at home."

"THAT'S why you want to leave? Because of your stupid phone?"

"Does anyone have an iPhone charging cable?" Declan calls out to the crowd.

No one answers.

"I'm pretty sure everyone here has an Android," I tell him.

"Why?"

"Because they're cheaper."

"What does cheap have to do with–oh."

"It's me, Shannon," Mom says, interrupting us. "He wants to leave because of *me*."

CHAPTER 12

One of the first character attributes I noticed in Declan, the day I met him in the men's bathroom at one of Anterdec's stores, my hand down the toilet as I retrieved my dropped cellphone, was his unflappable nature. It impressed me. Aroused me. Intrigued me.

Five years of being around my mother has really tested him.

But he stays cool.

"This has nothing to do with you, Marie."

"Then why?"

"I'm worried about the company. I'm..." His eyes jump around from Agnes to Jeffrey to Dad to me. "I need some time alone with Shannon."

Moving gracefully out of the way, Dad extends his arm as if to say, *This way, please.*

Declan moves us down the hall, into Carol's old room. It's trashed, two sleeping bags on the floor from where Jeffrey and Tyler slept last night, Carol's twin bed unmade, clothes everywhere.

Exactly what I'd expect from cramming a family of three into a room the size of a dorm single.

Neither of us cares about the mess.

"Shannon, I'm sorry."

Didn't expect that.

"You—are?"

"I'm struggling."

"You are?" My voice is softer, breaking slightly at the end, worry flooding me. "What's wrong?"

"I haven't had this much concentrated family time since..."

"Since your mother died."

"Yes. And, frankly, our family was never quite so—"

"Boisterous?"

"Chaotic."

"Ah. Well, even for us, this is a bit much. No one expected Agnes, Corrine, and Josh to— "

Ding dong!

Declan groans at the doorbell. "Who else?"

The door hinges creak as someone opens it. Suddenly, my father's very perplexed voice calls out:

"James?"

I gawk at Declan. "What's your father doing—"

"HAMISH!" Mom squeals as we hear big boots stomping on the foyer's tile floor. "What are *you* doing here?"

"So sorry to intrude, Marie. Uncle James said this would be the best option. I dinna have Declan's phone number in my new phone, and Uncle James said 'twould be fine to just—" A gaggle of voices blend together down the hall, making it hard to hear individual words, but it's clear that James and Hamish are being folded into the

Christmas morning celebration with fanfare and great cheer.

I have never, in five years with Declan, seen him disintegrate. It's extraordinary, really. I've seen him upset. Furious. Tearfully emotional. Lovingly protective.

But I have never seen him fall apart like *this*.

Sinking onto the edge of Carol's bed, he bends his head down, face in his hands, elbows on knees and takes in a long, slow, deep breath. Fingertips dig into his hairline, the contrast between his skin and dark hair mesmerizing. As he breathes, his shoulders broaden, widening as if to extend to carry a larger burden.

Then they collapse.

He's not crying. Dropping his suit of armor, he just melts, his body releasing the constant tension he holds inside him as a form of strength.

"I have my limits, Shannon. I'll never have this."

"Never have what?"

"What your family has. What they create. A part of me compares this to all that I know—my family life before I was seventeen."

"And it doesn't measure up? Is that what you're saying?"

"No! No," he says, grumpy and gruff, his words tinged with the only emotion he knows how to show when he's feeling too much. It's a layer I know he'll shed soon, the conversation we're having now just a preliminary to whatever's really going on inside him. "I'll never have it with my mother and my father and my siblings. I'm just another random stray your family has adopted."

"Oh!" My hand flies to my heart, the pain visceral. "No, no, Declan. It's not like that."

"Isn't it? I'll never have this with my family."

"That's not the point. You're missing the whole, big point."

"Which is?"

"You *do* have it. You *are* part of the family. You have been since the day we met, whether you knew it or not. This *is* your family."

"But—"

I bend before him and take his face in my hands, eyes narrowing to make sure he sees my intensity, not that I could stop it if I tried. "No buts. You are an extraordinary man, Declan. I would not be with you otherwise. And I love you dearly. I am not minimizing what you're feeling about your own family of origin. I'm not. But you have a family of creation—you, me, and Ellie. And our future children, too."

"Of course."

"You also have entered into my family. I chose you. We chose you. For the rest of your life, you will be connected to Mom, Dad, Carol, Jeffrey, Tyler, Amy—and whoever else we welcome into the family. You are family."

"I know, but—"

"No. You don't know. This is me telling you, you stubborn ass."

"Hey!" But he laughs, green eyes warm and tender, filled with a gratitude I've never seen in him. "If you're trying to make me feel better, calling me an ass isn't generally recommended."

"We have a marriage based on truth."

A long, strong sigh emerges from him as he presses his forehead against mine. "Yes. We do. Thank you."

"Being weak is part of life sometimes," I tell him.

"Who said I'm weak?" A smile accompanies his words.

"Vulnerable, then. Thank you for telling me how you feel."

"This is starting to sound like a therapy session, Shannon."

"No. This is just love."

"Where's the whiskey?" James calls out from the kitchen.

"That's my dad's idea of love. I can't believe he's here."

"It complicates the morning, doesn't it?"

"He complicates *everything*." The stoic look I know so well comes back to his features. "I'll manage."

Without invitation, I crawl into his lap, his warm arms embracing me like I'm a life preserver. He's dressed in a white button-down shirt with cuffs, the hem tucked into his jeans, all of the bumpy, crisp parts of him rubbing against my striped cotton pajamas. We don't interlock like puzzle pieces, but more like sundry items thrown into a bowl, each important but each individual.

Like emotions.

Declan's phone rings. He reaches calmly into his back pocket, holds it to his ear, and says, "Thanks for returning my call, Dave. Took you seven minutes. You're slipping."

"You called him on Christmas?" I burst out.

"Shannon has a point," Dave says flatly. I can hear the entire conversation because I'm leaning against Dec's shoulder. He doesn't shove me off, so I close my eyes and enjoy the quiet while I can.

"I need you to get me out of here."

"Sorry, I can't do that, Declan."

"How long have you been waiting to say that to me?"

"Longer than you could ever imagine."

"This isn't funny."

"Never said it was."

"I need to know what the roads are like."

"I hear 1030 WBZ has traffic on the threes."

"Not funny."

I snicker.

"Your wife thinks I am."

Declan broods.

"Fine, Declan. Bottom line is that the quick thaw will make roads easier to drive on, especially the interstates, by around five o'clock."

We look at the time. It's 8:30 a.m.

"But even then, branches could snap. HQ is fine. We have power there."

"What about our condo building?"

"Power's still on. But if it goes out, I have a team ready to clean out your fridge after the point of no return. I am monitoring the situation."

I raise my eyebrows and give Declan a thumbs up. Dave is good.

"Five p.m.? I'm stuck here for that long?"

"At least," Dave says calmly. "Nothing about the business is in jeopardy."

"Other than my sanity," Dec mutters.

"What's that?"

"You're telling me that as my executive assistant, whose job description is working miracles, you will not find a way to get me out of this mess?"

"Not *will not*. *Cannot*."

"The difference doesn't matter. Fix this."

"I can't change the weather."

"Can't or won't?"

"Now you're being hysterical."

"I am never hysterical."

"There's a first time for everything. May I request that you put Shannon on the phone now?"

A furious shade of red takes over Declan's face. "Why?"

"I'd like to speak with someone who hasn't abandoned logic in the face of a crisis."

"WHAT?"

"Uh, sure," I say, taking the phone out of Declan's rage-filled grip.

"I AM PERFECTLY LOGICAL!" my husband bellows, standing up suddenly. I roll onto the bed to avoid being dumped on the floor.

"Hi, Dave. Merry Christmas."

"It's just a consumerist holiday designed to turn us into debt slaves, Shannon."

"You should moonlight as Santa at the Ayn Rand Institute, Dave."

"Merry Christmas to you, too," he says, like a robot. "What can I do to help you?"

"Me? You don't work for me. You're Declan's assistant."

"I can help him best by helping you."

"I COULD FIRE YOU FOR THAT COMMENT!" Declan shouts.

Oh, dear.

Cupping my hand over the mouthpiece, I whisper to Dave, "Stop telling him he's not being logical."

"But he's not."

"I know that, and I know that, but he becomes irrational when you point out he's lost all sense of reason."

Dec hears me say that.

His nostrils flare. Hands turn to fists. The part of his

shirt that is open at the V turns a fiery red. "YOU TWO HAVE CROSSED A LINE!"

Tap tap tap.

"Shannon?" It's Dad, at the door. "Are you okay? Is that Declan who's yelling?"

"I'm fine!"

"Classic Declan." That's James's voice behind the door now. "I'm guessing he's hidden his explosive temper from all of you for years. Now you're getting a taste of what we lived with, raising him."

"Can you order a hit on his father?" I whisper into the phone.

"Before I answer that, I have one important question," Dave asks, all business.

"What?"

"Are you serious? Because once I begin the process, you can't take it back."

"JOKE!" I scream. "THAT WAS A JOKE!"

Dave sighs. "It seems your husband isn't the only hysterical one."

I smash my finger on the End button so hard I touch my own palm through the phone.

"Took you long enough to hang up on him," Declan fumes.

"Is he always like that?"

"Like what? Cold? Direct? Efficient?"

"Yes."

"He is. It's why he's too good to fire."

The door opens, Dad's worried face appearing, James behind him, giving us a condescending grin.

"Shannon was just screaming, too. What's going on in here?"

"Wild sex!" I chirp.

"You look just like Marie when you say that," Declan says, suddenly pale.

"Oh, God," James says, turning around and fleeing.

"But it worked," I tell my husband out of the corner of my mouth.

My dad is unfazed. Anyone who can be married to my mother for this long would have to be. "You two aren't hurting each other, are you?"

"Dad!"

"You said wild sex..."

"DAD!"

"Now *he* looks just like Marie," Declan groans.

"Whatever argument you're having, you might want to consider the fact that we still haven't opened presents, and Buggly Wuggly just peed all over Declan's boot."

"What is Buggly Wuggly?"

"Tyler's name for the dog."

"You're not seriously naming that puppy Buggly Wuggly?"

"No. We haven't decided. Marie's polling everyone, turning it into a game. Carol wants Woofus. Like Rufus. Amy's pushing for Puddles. Jeffrey's arguing for Puppy."

"Just Puppy?"

"He says it's ironic."

Declan runs a frustrated hand through his hair. "We'll be there shortly."

"You want a beer?"

"No. I need to stay sober in case I have to drive."

"In this? The governor's declared a state of emergency until 4 p.m."

"DAMN IT!"

"Geez. James was right. You *do* have a temper." Dad leaves, closing the door while winking at me.

Every relationship has a homeostasis level. You know what I mean. Expectations form pretty early as you take two individuals and forge a couplehood. One of you is more decisive than the other. One is more sensitive than the other. One is better with planning, while the other's more spontaneous. You know. Yin/yang and all that.

Declan is being emotional.

I am the emotional one.

I feel like he's appropriated a part of my identity and I'm standing here with a sucking chest wound.

Help.

"That's it!" Declan takes out his phone again and taps. I hear a phone ringing.

"Hello? Dec?" The voice is tinny but clear.

"Andrew! Is there power at your house?"

"Actually – "

"Wait. Damn. I forgot you're in Hawaii. Never mind."

"We're not. We're at home."

"What? Why? I thought you were in Hawaii!"

"Uh, we had a change of plans. In fact, we wanted to talk – "

Declan cuts him off. "Did the power go out there in Weston?" I'm so close, I can hear the conversation, just like with Dave.

Andrew clears his throat. "Yes, well, it did. But–"

Declan taps the End button.

"Why'd you hang up on him?" I ask, my voice going shrill. I clear my throat. His agitation is contagious. I have to find a way to manage my own.

"He said they don't have power. That's all I need to know."

"But that's rude!"

I'm clearly failing.

"You haven't seen rude yet."

Bee-boop! Declan's phone dies on the spot.

Remember that unflappable character trait?

It disappears.

Like his battery.

"What the hell is my father doing here?" Declan spits out.

"We have to leave this room to find out."

"I'm rethinking that beer."

"It's 8:30 in the morning!"

"Blame your dad."

"My dad?"

"He offered."

"I'm pretty sure he was joking."

"I'm not."

"Look, we can stand in here and argue all day, but I have to go get Ellie." I pat my breasts. "She hasn't nursed in a while and my breasts need some attention."

He leers at me.

"SERIOUSLY?" I shout, leaving him alone as I go into the cacophony of all the people.

Dec's on my heels, calling out, "Anyone have an iPhone charging cable? Dad? Hamish?"

"Sorry, son. I don't carry one of those." James gives me a quick hug and looks around the crazy, full living room. "Where's Ellie?"

We look down to find her eating the corner of a wrapped present.

"Mmmm, fiber," Hamish says, laughing heartily as he claps Dec on the back. I'm left to retrieve my baby, who is doing her best imitation of a mud dauber.

Why am I invoking wasps in my analogies? Ugh.

"iPhone charger?" Dec asks Hamish.

"Sorry. Android."

"What is wrong with all of you? Apple products are superior."

"Tastes great. Less filling," Dad mutters.

"Charge your phone in the Tesla," I tell him.

Hamish peeks outside and lets out a low whistle. "It's iced over."

"What are you *doing* here?" Dec demands of James, who gives him a half grin.

"That any way to greet your old man on Christmas?"

"*Please* tell me what you are doing here." Dec smirks. "Better?"

"Of course." And then they clap each other on the back like they're dislodging sputum. McCormick men don't do public displays of emotion.

The, er, American McCormick men, I mean.

"What a beautiful home! You've decorated in such a festive way, Marie. I love Christmas. Favorite time of the year. Makes me miss home and me mum's plum pudding," Hamish gushes, looking around the room like an excited golden retriever.

A six-foot-four, well-built, red-headed, blue-eyed, sports-modeling golden retriever.

Mom laps it up.

"Oh, Hamish, thank you so much! I consider that an honor from a man who seems to *truly* treasure family." Declan gets serious eye judgment from Mom as she says those words.

He doesn't notice.

Or care.

"It's so nice to have you drop in! We've already had breakfast, but I'm sure we can find something for you to eat!"

"We've had a bit already. I would love a good cup of tea, if you have any," he answers Mom.

"Of course!" Mom takes him to the kitchen, where Amy gawks as he walks by.

"What are *you* doing here?" she demands, grabbing his elbow as he passes.

He looks her up and down, her red and white pajamas really flattering her figure. "Looking for a sugarplum fairy. Seems I've found one. Those visions dancing in me head last night weren't fantasies, now, were they?"

He winks at her and walks away as Mom pulls out nineteen boxes of various teas. I hear the words *Earl Grey* and *Twining's* as Amy turns bright red, torn between anger and flattery.

"Take the compliment," I whisper at her.

"Why should I?"

"Because he's right."

"I'm hardly a sugarplum fairy. And what the hell is that, anyway? It's visions of sugarplums dancing in children's heads, and the sugarplum fairy is from Tchaikovsky's *Nutcracker*, so he's conflating two different cultural icons when he—"

I shove a donut hole in her mouth.

"THANNON!" she spits out.

"You sound like me, Auntie Amy!" Jeffrey giggles. "Before I outgrew my lisp!"

"Just chew, Amy." I sigh. "Just chew."

"Declan!" James calls out. "Can you believe the Worcester airport grounded my chartered jet? As if they have that kind of authority!"

"Uh, Dad, they do. That's *exactly* the kind of authority an airport has in cases of bad weather events."

James waves that idea away. "I'm filing a complaint with the FAA as soon as I'm home from St. Bart's."

Amy's eyes narrow as she swallows. "St. Bart's?"

"That's where Hamish and I are headed for the holiday. We were supposed to leave last night to be there for Christmas, but the weather did not cooperate."

"Who goes to St. Bart's for Christmas?" Amy's nose crinkles.

"People who don't wear matching pajamas," James shoots back.

"My mom made us do this!"

"A bit of advice, Amy: you are a grown woman. Your mother can't *make* you do anything."

"HAVE YOU MET MY MOTHER?" we ask in unison.

James looks Declan up and down. "Surely *you* didn't wear those silly pajamas?" He points towards Amy.

"What? No. Of course not," Dec lies.

Amy and I snicker. The truth will come out when Mom uses the photos she took earlier as next year's Christmas card. I know for a fact that James is on her list.

Let Declan have his 364 days of deception.

The truth always comes out.

Somehow, Mom shoos us all into the kitchen, where Corrine is standing in front of a huge carafe of coffee, every mug in the house spread out on the kitchen island. She pours, military style, so efficient, until the carafe's empty.

Then she starts to make a new pot.

Declan squints. "That coffee is so weak, it's amber."

"*Shhhhh.*"

He moves around her. She painstakingly adds a new filter to the machine and sprinkles exactly three flat scoops of coffee in there. Then, as she fills the carafe with water, Declan sneaks behind, adds five more, and slips away like a thief.

"Coffee?" Corrine asks, giving him a wink. Too polite to refuse, he takes the offered mug, but when she turns her back to him, Dec pours it into a ficus plant.

"Declan!" I hiss at him. "Won't that kill the tree?"

"Only if it dies from caffeine deprivation. That was homeopathic coffee Corrine just made."

"At least it wasn't entheogenic."

MIAAAOOOOWW! *PFFFFSSST!! HISS!!*

BARK! WOOF! *GRRR!!!*

Animal sounds come from the living room, where the presents are still clustered under the tree, Mom's half-assed baby gate set up to protect them from a puppy, a small bichon, a cat so angry, it belongs in the Michigan militia, and my almost-eight-month-old. Who is—thankfully—gumming freeze-dried strawberries right here in her high chair, looking like a baby vampire from the red juice running down her chin.

The puppy scoots under the tree. Chuckles gives chase, then climbs up the tree's trunk, in between the branches, and emerges at the top, next to the star.

Lunging, Chuckles takes a giant, flying leap in a surprise aerial attack on the dog.

Except—his collar gets caught on a firmly attached wire hook and he hangs at the tippy top for a few seconds, before physics and force and all that stuff I didn't understand in high school take effect. The entire tree crashes over, faster than you would think thanks to the weight of a twenty-pound cat. Chuckles is released at the end, zigzagging into the kitchen and making Corrine lose her balance and trip.

The glass of whiskey in her hand, kindly placed there by James, goes flying in an amber arc of glory, dousing the tree—now on the floor—and leaving a direct trail of alcohol into the fireplace. There's a hissing sound.

And the trail bursts into flame.

I grab Ellie from her high chair, instinct driving me to protect her. By the time I turn back around, the top of the tree, the carpet in front of the fireplace, and some of the presents are on fire, flames shooting up.

Ribbon makes a pretty display of glowing color when it *burns*.

"OUT! OUTSIDE NOW!" Dad bellows, pushing everyone out the kitchen's sliding door. "DECLAN! Fire extinguisher, coat closet!"

"I got it!" Amy screams. "Check upstairs for people!" she tells Dec, who runs up the staircase, shouting in case anyone's using the bathroom. It feels like hours, but in less than thirty seconds we've determined where everyone is; the cat, dog, and puppy are in the fenced yard; and Dad opens his man cave as Mom calls 911.

Amy, meanwhile, looks like Sigourney Weaver from the old *Aliens* franchise, except instead of using a flamethrower to kill alien eggs, she's whitewashing the Christmas tree.

Flames are out in seconds. Smoke, on the other hand, persists.

BEEE—oooooooo. BEEE—oooooooo.

Red lights flash within a minute. One freaking minute.

Dad runs back to the sliding glass door to help Corrine, who got up from tripping just fine, brandishing her cane with a smile. Whew. Let's not add a broken hip to this mayhem.

"How did they get here so fast?" Mom asks as we cram into the tiny shed, Dad offering his recliner to poor Agnes, who takes all of this in stride. Maybe when you're ninety-five, nothing's really an emergency anymore.

"They were down the road when I went for my walk!" Dad calls back.

"Why are we in your trash room?" James asks, looking at the faded upholstered recliner, Dad's sticker-covered dorm fridge, the exposed two-by-fours of the walls. "And did anyone grab the bottle of Scotch?"

"If you need alcohol, there's a beer fridge behind the television," Dad informs him before running around the left side of the house, skittering to a halt on a patch of ice.

Another set of sirens rings through the air, Carol covering Tyler's ears. An ambulance appears.

"Did the Christmas tree really catch fire?" Jeffrey asks as he grabs for Carol's phone. She hands it to him.

"Yes."

"COOL!" All the adults make contrary groans.

Crammed into this little space, I look around. Mom, Amy, Carol, Tyler, Jeffrey. Me, Ellie. Agnes. Corrine. James. Hamish.

"Where's Josh? And Declan?"

"Josh left ten minutes ago," Carol informs me. "Took the longest shower ever, used up all the hot water, and split. Not sure about Declan."

"DEC!" I shout.

He appears in the kitchen door and gives me a thumbs up. "I'm here. Amy put out the fire. But we've got company."

Hamish makes his way over to the door, bending considerably to get outside. "I'll help."

"Me, too," Amy announces.

"You stay with the rest," he assures her.

"That's sexist! I'm the one who put out the fire!"

He leans in and whispers, "You burned a hole in your shirt. It's melted to your bra. Someone needs to give ye a blanket. But I do like black lace."

She looks down. "Oh, my God!" Agnes tosses her a bar towel from the top of Dad's beer fridge, the Patriots logo landing right over her partly exposed boob.

Hamish disappears into the house.

"We're packed in like sardines!" Agnes says in a voice like sandpaper on gravel being run over by a steamroller. "But at least there's power!" She turns on a side-table lamp made from a quart beer bottle filled with aquarium pebbles. I think Carol made it in middle school.

"What about the presents? Did they burn? Mom, did you save the receipts?" a very worried Jeffrey asks Carol.

She smooths the lines of his brow with a thumb pad and smiles gently at him. "I'm sure it's fine, honey. Don't worry."

"But you said you weren't sure how we were going to manage the bills in January! And now—"

She pulls him in for a hug, more to shut him up in the crowd than to be comforting. "I said you don't need to worry, honey."

I make a mental note to follow up with her later on that bill thing.

"The presents are on fire," Tyler says somberly. "On fire for twenty-seven seconds."

"I'm sure it was longer," Corrine tells him.

"No! Twenty-seven seconds!" he insists.

"He's probably right. Tyler tends to notice exact stretches of time like that. It's a quirk he has."

"He'll make a wonderful engineer!" Corrine marvels.

"Or a great pimp," Agnes adds.

We all glare at her.

"ALL CLEAR!" a fireman shouts from the patio, his drab mustard outfit shaking me out of the stupor I'm in, making suppressed panic flood into my limbs. Fire trucks are at my mom and dad's house on Christmas morning. The tree caught fire. Presents, too.

There was a fire. My baby was in a *fire*.

My heart starts slamming in my chest, the air too thin to be enough in my lungs, my shoulders rising and falling as I take shallow breaths that feel like I'm drowning. Ellie's still in my arms, quiet but observant, and I hold her to me as I gulp in air, shivering though it's now stifling in the shed.

"Shannon?" Corrine's bony hand on my shoulder makes me turn, the intrusion of cold, hard connection shaking me out of my hysteria for a few seconds. "You're shaking horribly, and you look like you're about to faint." She's firm, worried, and her arms reach out. "Give me the baby and sit down. Agnes, get your Zamboni pancake ass up off that chair."

"I'm fine." But I hand off Ellie and fold my arms around myself.

Carol reaches for me, hands on my shoulders, forcing eye contact. "It's okay. The fire department's here. Amy put out the fire. We're all fine."

"I know." I can't stop shaking.

She leans in and whispers, "It's all different when you have a child, isn't it? You run through the worst-case scenarios and... it's different."

"Yes. I mean, it also became different when I met Declan. Suddenly, I had more to lose than just me."

"Come on in!" calls out a different fireman, this one with an oddly familiar voice. He's not wearing the mustard-yellow suit, but a different navy-blue uniform. I flash Carol a grateful smile and take a cooing Ellie back from Corrine.

The house smells like burnt pine, bad coffee, and thick smoke as we file in.

"I know you!" says the fireman, a young guy who is really alarmingly familiar. He's standing next to another guy, and I realize they're paramedics. Donny and Chip are the names on their uniforms.

"Do you… have we met?" Chip. *Chip*. Where have I heard that name?

"I know!" he says, snapping his fingers. "You must have come into my restaurant!"

"Restaurant?" Declan asks, putting his arm around my waist in a show of comfort and—*of course*—territoriality.

"Oh, right! Chip." Memories of my lunch with Amanda flood me suddenly. I realize my error, but it's too late to pull back now.

The O Spa joke. Husband swapping. He's from Upton. Oh, no.

"Are you—are you testing that new product?" He winks at me. "You've got quite a crowd."

Declan gives me a questioning look, except he's so annoyed from not understanding what's going on that he just looks like he's about to eat my face. "What product? Were you doing market testing out *here* on the new product program?" He looks at Chip. "I'm Declan McCormick. CEO. Her husband."

My mouth can't keep up with my racing brain. What have I done? I *told* Amanda it was a small world! And Chip seems to remember every part of that ridiculous conversation.

"So—so your husbands *know* about it?" Chip squeaks. "Seriously?"

"Of course I know about it! I'm the buyer!" Declan booms.

"Buyer!" Chip's voice goes low. "You... you *buy* the product she's selling?"

"I buy all of the product."

I rub Declan's back affectionately. "He's an integral part of the business, of course."

"But that's slavery!"

"What? No! We have no slavery on our plantations," Declan corrects him.

"YOU HAVE PLANTATIONS FOR WHAT YOU DO?" Chip shrieks at me. "You are a sick, sick woman! You need to let those poor men go!"

"Why is this guy losing it over coffee plantations?" Declan whispers in my ear as Ellie grabs a fistful of exposed chest hair at his collarbone and yanks. Hard.

"I don't know. What were you saying about trying to leave?" I ask him nervously.

"Just got a text. The airport is up and running again," James announces, turning to Chip. "How much for you to get me back to Worcester?" He eyes the ambulance. "That looks sturdy enough to make it through."

"How much? I don't understand."

"Fine. $500."

"You want to pay me *five hundred dollars* to take you to the regional airport?"

"No. To clear the way."

"You want me to clear a path to 495 so you can get to the Pike and then to Worcester?"

"Yes. I've had a lovely time with my son and grand-daughter, but I have business to attend to."

Notice who he left out of that? Blood is always thicker than anything–even whiskey–when it comes to James.

"And what's your business?"

"A fine resort in St. Bart's."

Chip crosses his arms over his chest and pointedly looks at Declan and me. "What *kind* of resort?"

"Why does that matter?"

"Is it one of these plantations your son is running? Where they grow the husbands?"

Declan freezes. He blinks once. His eyes narrow. "Excuse me?"

Chip points to me. "I know all about what you people do. She told me you're in the business of husband swapping!"

Slowly, every pair of eyes in the room swivels to me, long before their brains catch up to their vision's effort to pinpoint the source of Chip's claim. It's a painful process, all those orbs fixating on me, their heads turning, ears tilting to hear whatever answer I have to spontaneously generate. It has to make sense. It must defuse.

And most important: it has to be eloquent.

"I'm gonna kill Amanda," is the best I can come up with.

"Because her husband is better in bed than yours?" Chip asks sincerely.

Declan gives me a look that says, well—I have no idea what it says, because I can't hear anything over the sound of every atom in the universe collapsing in on itself and rushing through my bloodstream. It's like the Dawg Pound at every Browns game has taken up residence inside my liver.

But I have to say *something*.

"This, uh, isn't what you think," I start as Declan turns into a furnace before my very eyes.

"Oh, honey," Mom whispers. "That line never works. Trust me."

"Seven hundred and fifty dollars! That's my final offer!" James blusters.

Chip's eyes light up. "Make it a thousand and you've got a deal."

"*I'll* drive you to the airport for free, James!" I call out, hastily making my move. "You know. Family first! Let's go right now! Chop chop!"

"So that's how it is in this family," Chip says in a knowing voice. "Like that conversation you had with your sister-in-law about those brothers you married and the swap–"

I move fast, but Dec's reflexes are faster. Damn those fast-twitch muscles of his that he exercises six times a week with personal trainers. He grabs my arm and steers me into a soot-filled corner.

"What the hell is going on?"

"I'll explain later."

He crosses his arms over his chest, feet rooted in place. "Now."

"It–it was a joke."

"Of course it was. Everyone knows I'm better in bed than Andrew."

"How would 'everyone' know–"

"Shannon." Low and threatening, his voice carries a tone that shuts me up.

"It was–Amanda and I had lunch at a restaurant in Boston. Chip was the waiter. We were goofing around. We joked about the O Spa running a husband-swapping program."

"Your idea of humor leaves much to be desired."

"Come on! We were just being silly."

"You expect me to believe that your waiter in Boston happens to be an EMT one town over?"

"Boston is really just a small town pretending to be a large metropolitan city, Dec."

"Goodbye!" James shouts at the front door, Hamish next to him. "We have procured assistance and as lovely as it's been visiting, we're on our way to a real Christmas celebration! I prefer mine where the tree doesn't double as a Yule log!"

Dad rushes over to the door. "Hold on!"

"Why?" James looks righteously ruffled.

"Look, man, I haven't re-salted out there. You need to hold onto Hamish's arm on the walk to the car."

"I *what?*"

"You need help. I don't want you breaking a hip on my walkway."

James snorts. "As if I would bother suing *you!*" He looks around the house with disdain.

Dad reddens, jaw clenching. "I wasn't talking about money. I was talking about your health and wellbeing."

"Why would you care about that?" James huffs, moving past Dad as Hamish finishes saying his goodbyes. Down the steps James goes, then onto the sidewalk.

One.

Two.

Three.

Four.

"AAAAUGGHH!" James shouts as, sure enough, Dad was right. Feet up, hands down, head curled in, James does a remarkable chin tuck and lands, thankfully, with his head on the ice-covered grass, hips and legs on the ice-covered concrete walk.

"You called it, didna ye?" Hamish says to Dad as he hustles outside to help.

"Thank God for the ambulance," Agnes says, standing behind me. She rattles her walker. "Does that old man need this?"

"Old man?" James shouts in fury. But he can't stand. Loud groans of pain make me sympathetic as Declan joins Hamish, the two working to right my father-in-law and get him in a safe space.

Chip sighs. "Guess I'm just driving you to the hospital," he mutters, walking out to the vehicles, his shoe grips making it easy.

"And I guess I'm going on that trip, too," Declan says with a resigned groan. I'm on the welcome mat now. Carol grabs my hand.

"I've got Ellie under control. You help them." She disappears back into the house.

"I am fine!" my not-fine father-in-law insists. Dec and Hamish get him to a standing position, but James has gone white as a sheet and looks like he can't put pressure on his right leg.

"Dad, we need to get you to a hospital."

"I am *fine*, Declan! I just need to walk it off."

"Hip fractures at our age are a real humdinger!" Corrine calls out, waving her cane.

"*Our?*" James says, incredulous. "Does she think I'm anywhere near her age?"

Diplomacy is a McCormick family trait. How do I know? Because both Hamish and Declan keep their mouths shut.

"I'll go with Uncle James," Hamish says under his breath. "You stay. Unless you want a reason to leave?"

"If I were looking for a reason to leave, going to a

hospital with my dad on Christmas wouldn't be top of my list."

"Mine either, son. Mine either," James mutters.

"This is your daughter's very first Christmas, cousin. You need to be here with her and your wife. I'll help Uncle James."

"That's very kind of you, Hamish, but—"

"No buts." He leans in and whispers, "Or perhaps it's because of butts."

"What?"

Jutting his chin, Hamish points to Agnes and Corrine. "I need to get out of here. This place is crazy. Those old ladies won't stop with the grabby hands."

Before Declan can argue—and trust me, Declan *wants* to argue—Hamish is next to the ambulance and helping James in.

"You drive the car," he insists to Hamish, who eyes the new red Jaguar James bought last summer.

"Of course," he says as James hands over the keys.

"Wait. Have you ever driven on ice?" Declan calls out to him.

Auburn eyebrows climb like he's bagging a Munro. "I might be from Edinburgh, but I've driven in other parts of Scotland plenty of times. Of course I've driven on ice! Whadda ye take me fer?" He climbs into the car with relish, waving goodbye as he starts the engine.

I watch as Chip closes the ambulance's rear doors and walks to the front, shaking his head. The other guy, Donny, looks at him. They exchange words. Donny starts laughing.

And then so does Dad.

CHAPTER 13

"*T*hat stubborn old bastard," Dad chokes out through rueful laughter.

"Hey!" Declan says.

"Jason!" Mom gasps.

"Am I wrong?" Dad asserts, locking eyes with Declan.

We all shrug. One corner of Dec's mouth turns up in a half snarl, half-reluctant acknowledgment that Dad has a point.

"I tried to warn him. Now he's on his way to the ER."

"No." Declan's voice is tinged with disgust. "He's not. He'll pay them off. Get an escort to the airport. By the time they hit 495, he'll have negotiated a deal in his favor."

"Municipal ambulances don't work like that, Declan."

"James McCormick *does* work like that, Jason. Trust me."

"He really thinks the rules don't apply to him, doesn't he? That fall had to hurt. Think he broke something?"

"Only a tiny corner of his ego."

"Given it's the size of a glacier, he'll be fine."

"Besides," I tell Dec, who looks more troubled than I'd

expect over his father's accident, "Hamish is with him. I'm sure he'll call you if something's really wrong."

"You mean he'll call me from the beach in St. Bart's?"

"You really think they're going straight to the airport, don't you?"

"I know they are. That's Dad. The second he showed up here, I knew he would find a way to manipulate this."

"You think he made the firefighters come? You think he set the tree on fire?"

"No, no. That was all Chuckles. But Dad found a way to turn it to his advantage."

"I guess that's why he's a billionaire and I'm not," my father says with a smug laugh. The words sound like a pity party on paper, but in real life, they're a weapon.

Against James.

Dec pulls me aside.

"We need to leave. Now."

"You want to abandon my parents and family like this?"

"I think we're just adding to the confusion, Shannon. This is nuts. Let's go home and we can invite them over tomorrow, if you really need a bigger dose of 'family.'"

The way he says that word–*family*–can go either way. My ears want to hear contempt, but something about him is more contemplative.

"And our place doesn't have melted, charred carpet, a tree that looks like a burnt marshmallow stick at a campfire, and Agnes."

"It's not safe to drive! And where can we go? What about the electricity?"

"Home. There's power, according to Dave. It's central Mass that was hit hardest. Let's get *home*."

"But the roads are a mess!"

"Not the major ones. I-495 and the Mass Pike are salted and clear," he argues.

"But the side roads! I don't want to get in an accident. We have Ellie."

"We have an SUV. The major roads are fine."

"We could get hurt."

"Pretty sure that's happening here."

"It's not that bad."

"Agnes and Corrine have taken over your father's man cave."

"Oh, no."

"They're calling it the Land of Estrogenphalia and insisting that *Winter is Coming*."

"That's a pretty clever pun on *Game of Thrones*. Get it? Estrogen-fail... They're pretty hip, aren't they?" My nervous voice winds down as his eyes go dull.

"Shannon." His voice is a demand, a plea, a sacrifice, a prayer, all at once.

"Yes?"

CRACK!

As if God him—or her—self reached down with one almighty hand and ripped the giant branch off the old oak in the front yard, slamming it to the ground like a WWF wrestler, we hear an enormous noise, thousands of smaller twigs shattering like spun glass.

And the house goes quiet.

The lights flip off, the hum of the furnace ends, the fridge's motor dies. It's completely silent, the kind that makes your ears ring.

All of the inflatable decorations on the front lawn slowly deflate, melting into fabric pools of failure on the ice. They go limp and lifeless, disturbingly devoid of the fun and frolic they represented.

It's almost worse than losing electricity. That tree branch doesn't just take away the power to the house.

It cuts off our supply of Christmas cheer.

"Huh," Declan says under his breath. "Reminds me of the night we started trying to conceive."

"What?"

"Nothing. Never mind," he says quickly.

Tyler starts to cry from the backyard, where he's still in the man cave.

"What do we do now?" Amy calls out. Sunlight still streams in. There's plenty of natural light. It's not even ten a.m., so we're fine until the grid can be restored.

Dad moves to the front door again and looks outside.

"Line to the house is down. Damn it! That's our responsibility."

"What does that mean?" Dec asks.

"Means the power's still on at the road. That tree branch knocked out the line from the road to the house. We have to call an electrician to come and restore it." Dad's face falls, bright-blue eyes going sad. "They're swamped, and it's Christmas. We'll be on a waiting list a mile long."

"Can't we fix it?" Jeffrey asks from behind me. "Get a ladder and do it, Grandpa? Like when we fixed the cable dish?"

Declan gives Dad a hopeful look for a brief second before reality sinks in. "No," Dad says. "Can't touch a live wire like that. Even I have my DIY limitations."

Dad frowns and looks at Declan. "I know you want to leave."

"No. We'll stay. You're going to need help. If you have a chainsaw, we can clear that, and–"

"Actually, I was thinking the opposite. First of all, I

won't go near that branch when it's pinning a wire down. Second, the house is a burned mess, but Marie and I can handle that. Carol, Jeffrey, and Tyler are fine here, or they can walk home by mid-afternoon. I'll have Agnes call her daughter and see what they want to do. But you have the baby, and I heard on the radio that Boston has more power."

"Yes. Sounds like our place is fine." Declan gives him a resigned smile. "Want to move Christmas there?"

"No, no. Have to be here and make sure pipes don't burst, handle the mayhem, you know..." He laughs. "This is one Christmas for the record books." Chuckles cozies up to Dad's legs and purrs, looking up as if to say, *Feed me, you stupid human.*

"And you!" Dad says to him, looking down. "You're the one who caused this mess!"

Chuckles doesn't blink.

"We'll take him home, too. And we'll pay for all the damage," I insist.

"Of course," Declan joins in, his words a rush. "Goes without saying."

"YOU CAN'T LEAVE!" Mom screams at the top of her lungs from the vicinity of the Christmas tree, where she's sorting through presents to see what can be salvaged.

"Mom, you're covered in fire extinguisher... stuff. What's that called again?"

"It looks like marshmallow fluff," Declan says.

"Looks more like a bukkake film," Carol whispers in my ear.

"NOT FUNNY!" I shriek.

Even Declan snorts, though.

"I KNOW IT'S NOT FUNNY! It's never funny when my children want to leave a big family event!" Mom sobs.

"That's not what I—never mind," I hastily say, definitely not wanting to explain Carol's joke to Mom. "Dad thinks it's better if we take Ellie home, where there's power. I think he's right."

"You do?" Declan's surprised.

"I do." I look at Carol. "It's different when you have kids."

"YES, IT IS!" Mom screams.

"That's not what I—"

Declan goes upstairs and comes back with our bags completely packed, shrugging into his coat. "Okay. Ready."

"I need to change!" I protest.

He hands me our bag. "Here. Go change. I'll get Ellie's snowsuit."

Five minutes later, we're assembled in the foyer, ready to go.

Ten minutes later, we're still giving goodbye hugs and kisses with promises to have everyone over to our house tomorrow or the twenty-seventh.

Eight minutes after that we realize we've forgotten to give Agnes and Corrine hugs and goodbyes, and...

That's right.

It takes *forty-two minutes* to hug, kiss, talk to, extract promises from, make promises to, accept plates of cookies from Mom, offer condolences to my nephews for their burnt presents, let people kiss Ellie's chubby cheeks yet again, corral Chuckles twice into the carrier, and generally extract ourselves from my parents' house.

Welcome to my family.

Safely in the car, secured by our seatbelts, I turn to Declan as he fiddles with the heat. My eyes nervously take in the defrosting windshield, Ellie in her carseat, and the broken tree branches we gingerly work around on our way out of here. The sun is gleaming, heating everything up nicely but making the roads a dangerous combination of wet and frozen.

A salt truck came by, so the street seems fine as Declan slowly backs out of the driveway.

We move forward.

We don't slip.

Success!

Until we're on I-495 north, Dec and I don't say a word, Ellie unnaturally quiet in the backseat, as if she understands how stressful the day has already been and she's so emotionally intelligent she just gets it. The interstate is remarkably clear, but then again, it's Christmas morning and the governor told people to stay home.

A rush of trepidation comes over me.

"Declan? Maybe we should go back. The governor declared a state of emergency and–"

"No."

I go quiet.

Ellie, on the other hand, has some opinions to share.

"DA DA DA DA DA DA DA DA DA!!!!!!"

We're serenaded with this lovely chorus until we reach the turn for I-90 east, the Mass Pike looming ahead.

"Roads are fine," Declan mumbles to himself.

"MUH MUH NUH NUH MUH MUH NUH NUH!"

"Ellie's not." I say it with exaggerated enunciation, the universal signal that *I'm* not, either.

"She's fine." He handles the cloverleaf, gets into the straightaway, and goes about fifty, moving carefully. Full sunshine makes a difference, the road feeling fine and looking dry.

Then it hits me.

Today is Christmas.

It's not even noon.

I didn't get to see my nephews open their gifts. Mom, Dad, Carol, or Amy, either.

My baby's first Christmas involved the tree catching on fire.

People think I'm into husband swapping.

And maybe worst of all, I'm caffeine deprived beyond belief.

Breathing slowly, I try not to sob. I really do. The well-spring of emotion hits me all at once, Ellie's pleas for MUH MUH NUH NUH making my breasts tingle, my stomach churning, all of me reliving the last few hours in a blur of *WTF just happened?*

"Oh, honey," Declan says, his voice filled with the first sign of deeper connection to me in what feels like forever.

"I–I–I can't believe this is my baby's first Christmas! This! Mom lit a penis candle, Agnes and Corrine were there cracking jokes about asses, your dad may have broken his hip, the tree caught on fire–"

"MEOW," Chuckles says.

"At least he's trying to apologize," Declan notes.

"I think that was a declaration of victory," I say through hitched breath.

"MUH MUH NUH NUH!!!!!" Ellie screams. "Kih kih!!!"

"She... wants me to nurse Chuckles?"

"If you did, it wouldn't be the weirdest thing that happened today."

Full-blown crying starts in Ellie, her face turning red.

"Is she crying because I'm crying?" I beg Declan, asking for an answer he can't give. "I know babies are emotionally attuned to their parents, but–oh, my God! I have to stop crying!"

I cry harder.

Ellie brings it up a notch.

That makes me cry even harder.

Then Chuckles starts to make a strange sound, like a strangled baby in the distance.

"STOP IT!" I gasp at the cat, the sound unnerving.

"TOP IT!" Ellie shouts. "TOP IT! TOP IT!"

"If you say that's another new two-word sentence," I warn Declan, "I'm going to set *our* Christmas tree on fire when we get home."

"Why would you say such a thing?"

"Because I have absolutely zero control over my emotions right now."

And then Declan asks the wrong question.

"You're not pregnant again, are you? Because you acted just like this before you–"

"DA DA UM BUH! DA DA UM BUH!"

"NO! I'm not pregnant! STOP IT!"

"TOP IT! TOP IT!"

Inhaling slowly, Declan gives his full attention to the road, exactly where it should be. I lean back against the cool, soft leather of the seat and make myself close my eyes, willfully tuning out Ellie's cries. It's not because I don't care, or from a lack of compassion.

It's because I have to put on my oxygen mask before I can put hers on.

A few deep breaths later and I open my eyes, twisting in my seat to try to get her attention. Hysterical hiccups and rhythmic screaming are all Ellie is producing.

I start singing to her, a favorite lullaby.

Nope.

I find the bubble container in the diaper bag at my feet and blow some in the backseat.

Nope.

As the road improves and Declan takes the car up to sixty, her cries become even more panicked, making something flutter inside my chest, as if my heart is trying to escape and pick her up to soothe her.

"Dec, can we stop? She sounds like she's in pain."

A terse nod. "Next exit."

Except... within one mile, we see a ton of police cars blocking the road, blue and red flashing lights forming a literal wall.

Declan turns on news radio, the familiar tones of WBZ 1030 filling the car.

"*... massive accident on the Pike, with possible fatalities, a seven-car pile up. All eastbound traffic is being re-routed via the Weston tolls...*"

"Fatalities!" I gasp. "On Christmas?" Instant tears fill my eyes.

"Maybe this was a bad idea," he mutters. "I–I hope I wasn't being too stupid."

I can't hear the exact words he says after that, Ellie's cries drowning everything out.

"We need to stop."

"Where? It's Christmas, Shannon."

"We're being forced off at Route 30, right? Weston?"

"Yes."

"Can we go to Andrew's?"

"We're only half an hour from home."

"I don't think Ellie can handle another half hour. We're ten minutes from Andrew and Amanda. Let's just go there." Snaking through the backed-up traffic, he moves along the police-guided line, creeping up to the stop light, turning right.

Ellie's screams stop abruptly. A loud, explosive sound from her diaper follows, then even more screaming.

"Oh, no," I say, avoiding eye contact with Declan for no reason whatsoever.

"Got it. Seven minutes left. Can she hold out?"

"I think we're going to need a bath for her."

Singing her favorite lullaby over and over has no discernible positive effect on my baby, but it's something I can do. So I sing. As Declan turns off Route 30 and we wind down back roads, I eye the asphalt with worry.

"Are you sure these country roads are safe?"

"Country roads?" He laughs. "Weston is hardly rural."

"It's all winding, wooded land."

"I'll bet Andrew kept Dad's deal with the local sand-and-plow guy."

"Deal?"

"Dad always paid some townie a big pile of money to make the drive between the house and the Pike clear before any other section of road."

"He bribed a town employee? Isn't that highly illegal?"

"No. Just some local plow guy."

"So you're sure it's safe?"

We're talking to each other above Ellie's cries, and it's killing me, but this is a part of parenting I'm becoming increasingly familiar with: the part where you just slog through, because there is no alternative. If we pull over and calm her down, we could get into a bigger mess. In the grand scheme of things, seven minutes isn't that long.

To a screaming infant who wants her mommy, it's forever.

And it feels like eternity to Mommy, too.

Two minutes later, we're turning left into Andrew and Amanda's driveway. I let out a sigh of relief, until Declan slams on the brakes so suddenly, the car careens to the left and slides at a diagonal–

Towards an enormous fallen oak tree that is blocking the entire driveway.

"Holy shit!" Declan shouts as we come to a halt. Thankfully, we don't hit the huge trunk, but we're so close that I can see the bark's detail.

The curtains in a front window move as Pam's face looks out, then fall into place again.

My heart feels like it's on the dashboard, trying to crawl into the engine.

"MAMAMAMAMAMAMAMAMAMAMAMAMAMA-MAAAAAHHHHHHHHHHHHHHHH!" Ellie screams, now absolutely terrified. I unclick my seat belt and get out, pleased to find the ground unevenly sanded, but enough to walk on safely. I open the back car door and unclick her, ignoring the stench, holding her close against my shoulder, her body relaxing.

"Here," Dec says, tossing me a thick fleece blanket, which I put over her. My hand sinks into the obvious cause of her distress, a diaper blowout.

"DECLAN?" Andrew shouts, approaching us as he slides his arm into a parka. "What are *you* doing here?"

For the first time, I look at the house. *Really* look at it.

Every window is lit with a single electric candle, in the classic New England holiday tradition. An evergreen tree growing on the lawn is wrapped in tiny white lights. Inside the house, I can just make out what appears to be a huge, illuminated Christmas tree in the living room.

The house is well lit.

They have power? Out here?

"Hey!" Declan calls out. "We need help! Ellie's with us and–"

Amanda stands on the wide porch and shouts, "Come on in! Get out of the cold!"

Dec grabs the diaper bag and gets our overnight bag and Chuckles' carrier from the back. Andrew has reached the fallen tree and takes the baggage from Declan, who helps me climb over the huge trunk with Ellie. We trudge up the steps and the four of us head inside, Dec peppering Andrew with questions.

Or, rather, angry outbursts.

"You have power! Why didn't you tell me when I called?"

"I tried to, but you hung up on me."

"And you didn't call back?"

"I did! You have about ten voicemails from me. You never returned them!"

"My phone died."

Andrew laughs in victory. "Ever hear of a charging cable?"

Dec's mouth tightens.

"Then we tried to call you," Amanda says to me, "but yours went right to voicemail, too. Did you turn it off?"

"Oh, no," I answer in a small voice. "It died yesterday and we didn't have a charging cable and – "

"None of that matters now," Andrew says as he gives me a worried look. "You're here. We have lights and heat and plenty of food. You guys came all the way from Jason and Marie's house? Did they lose power?"

"Yes," Declan says.

"No," I say.

"Which is it?"

"They had power, but then they lost it," I explain. "And James hurt himself, but he–"

Andrew interrupts. "James? *Dad* was at your parents' house?"

"Yes. With Hamish," Dec explains.

"I–you spent Christmas with Dad?" Jealousy oozes out of Andrew's surprised words. "And no one told me?"

"Trust me. It wasn't like that," Declan replies.

"He called us last month and asked if we would come to St. Bart's."

"Was that the phone call when Amanda and I were at lunch? He called."

"Probably," Andrew tells me. "But when he knew we were going to Hawaii, he just..." His voice trails off. He gives Declan a confused look. "Why was he at Jason and Marie's house?"

"Because Worcester grounded his chartered jet to St. Bart's and Dad knew we were nearby."

"And he got hurt?"

"Slipped on the ice."

I walk away as Declan fills him in, to be greeted by a warm and beaming, but clearly concerned, Amanda. "What happened?"

"Ellie needs a hose and a decontamination chamber. Me, too."

She sniffs. "Oh, dear." Heading straight for a bathroom, she stops, turns around and takes the diaper bag from Declan, then catches up to me as I set Ellie down on the wide, long counter in the bathroom.

"What happened? I mean, of course you're welcome here, and we love the company. But I thought you were in Mendon with your family?"

"It's a long story." Ellie has calmed down, thank goodness, but she decides this is a great time to do her best impression of a greased pig.

Except that's *not* grease.

Amanda plugs the sink and starts running the water, the extra-wide basin just big enough to put a filthy baby in it for a bath. We work together so seamlessly. I'm grateful.

Amanda's going to make a wonderful mother someday.

Our eyes meet. She's a little green. Her hand goes to her mouth. "I, uh, need to leave you to this part."

And with that, she skedaddles.

Huh. That's weird. But she got me this far, so without further ado, I wipe as much off Ellie as I can, then plunk her in the shallow water that's already in the sink.

She looks up at me, red face streaked with tears, fluffy dark hair around her ears, and beams. Her little fingers encircle mine and she squeezes.

I sigh. My back releases all the tension I've been holding. Sunny outside, the world feels different here. Ellie splashes, her flat palms catching plenty of water as she giggles.

From crying to laughter in just a few minutes.

Ah, life.

I use some hand-pump soap to wash Ellie, figuring her hair and face are fine as is, and soon I have a happy baby in a fresh diaper and a clean red velvet jumper.

I, on the other hand, feel about as fresh as a crumpled bag in a trash can after a Pats game at Gillette Stadium.

Pam appears in the doorway and reaches for Ellie with even more enthusiasm than usual. I guess everyone can see how stressed out we all are. To my surprise, Ellie settles down instantly as Pam shushes her, bobbing up and down to keep her happy. From her easy movement, I can tell that Pam's fibromyalgia isn't flaring up today.

"I just love babies," Pam says, her voice suddenly filled with extraordinary emotion.

The hair on the back of my neck stands tall, like an eighth-grade cheerleader watching the last five seconds of the clock before halftime.

"Where's Amanda?" I ask, holding back on all the facial expressions I know will leak through as suspicion awakens in my mind.

"In the kitchen. But she said you and Declan should take your time. I've got Ellie."

"Take our time?"

"Relax, and maybe... shower?" Pam eyes the front of me with a level of restrained politeness that makes me look down.

Oh, shit.

No. Really. I'm the victim of a diaper-plosion. I peel off my cardigan and sling it over my arm. Nothing got through to my shirt, thank goodness.

Ah, motherhood. So much glamour.

"That sounds good, actually." Declan pokes his head in, Andrew and Amanda behind him in the hall. He holds up our overnight bag. "I brought everything in."

"Use our bathroom," Andrew offers. "It has the double shower *and* the tub."

"A bath sounds amazing, but I can't. Ellie needs—"

"*Shhhhhh.*" Pam's finger is across her lips. Ellie is asleep on her shoulder, little rosebud lips sucking on an imaginary breast.

"How did you get her to fall asleep so fast?" I whisper.

"Magic touch. I guess I've still got it."

Amanda gives her a heartfelt smile. "Good," she says. The two share a deeply emotional look.

Mmm hmmm.

My bestie is up to something. "Amanda, I–"

"Come on," Declan interrupts me, taking my hand. "Let's go."

"But I want to ask Amanda why they didn't go to Hawaii. And why Pam's acting all – "

"Ask later." The pull of his grip overrides anything I can ask, and soon we're upstairs in Andrew and Amanda's master suite. Declan strips his clothes off and piles them neatly on their bed. He strides into the bathroom, turns on the shower, and a loud sigh of pleasure fills the space.

My bones are slower than his.

I follow him into the bathroom, expecting to run a bath, but I jolt and change plans on the spot. The sight of my nude, wet husband under multiple shower heads in an increasingly steamy shower is so appealing. Not just in a sexual way. More like a sanctuary. We're tired and over-wrought, and the opportunity to focus on something as banal as getting clean is appealing.

So is Declan.

I drop my filthy cardigan on the wood floor at the edge of a gorgeous wool rug and strip down, mirroring Declan's movements. Steam has now filled the shower, Dec's presence detected only by the appearance of an elbow, fingers that brush against the now-opaque glass, a glimpse of hands moving up to shampoo his dark hair. Slipping in like a thief of intimacy, I find him, wet and slippery.

His hungry hands find my body like he was expecting me.

"I'm sorry," we say in unison. Declan moves us just out of the path of the strongest shower stream, the jets set to rib height warming me through and through. Declan's touch helps, too.

"This day did not go as planned," he says before

kissing me, long and full, sweet and unhurried. The disjointed feeling of still being half back at Mom and Dad's and half here, present in my husband's naked arms as we move like spirits in the mists fades to a complete and utter wholeness. Right here, right now.

"No," I whisper into his wet ear, eyes taking in the dark curve of it against the back of his neck. "It didn't. But as long as I'm with you, none of it matters."

"I was a jerk."

"So was I. But we're here. No one got hurt. Christmas is about being with family. Just... we're not with the family I thought we'd be with," I say with genuine laughter.

He smiles down at me, water turning the tips of his eyelashes into something young and pure, the feel of his palms on my back like being touched for the first time. Water pools between us where our skin touches, belly to belly, thigh to thigh. He's hard against me and I'm soft and yielding, the kiss we share going deeper, bolder, harder and so much more as I reach up, cupping the back of his wet head, his hands splayed flat against my shoulder blades, making me breathless.

"Merry Christmas, Shannon," he whispers as our lips touch, cheek to cheek, his hands sliding up, making me gasp.

"Merry Christmas, Declan. I love you."

"I love you, too."

And we show each other exactly how much.

CHAPTER 14

*F*reshly dressed and definitely less stressed, we come downstairs to find the coziest sight, like an IKEA commercial and the Hallmark Channel joined forces and went Full Christmas Cheesy Charm.

Pam is in a wingback chair near the fire, Ellie still asleep on her shoulder, her teacup chihuahua Spritzy in her lap, chin on her knee, a sentry of sorts.

Amanda and Andrew are curled up together on the sofa, both drinking what smells like hot cider with cinnamon.

On a small table near the entrance, I spot my phone plugged in to a charging cable Andrew or Amanda must have lent us. "Did you find my dead phone in the diaper bag?"

She gives me a lazy nod.

It's charged just enough for me to try to call Mom. No answer. I try Dad. No answer. Just as I'm about to call Carol, a text buzzes on my phone.

We're fine, Dad says. *Fire's roaring, Marie found the old camp stove and I fired up the grill. Grilling the turkey and ham now. Glad you're safe. We'll take Declan up on the offer to come tomorrow to your place.*

I'll wait a few hours before telling Declan *that*.

I text back my love and set the phone down, glass side touching the table top. I need to pull back into Declan's arms right now and let my nerves settle.

What a day.

The fire roars beautifully, unneeded because I can hear the furnace in the distance. A tree occupies one whole corner of the room, hung with what look like old family ornaments and ablaze with twinkling lights.

"How did you keep power? That tree in the driveway must have taken out the line. That's what happened at my parents' house. We woke up to power but lost it later when a huge branch came down." I sit down in a deep, soft velvet chair across from Amanda and Andrew, sinking in with pleasure. I'm finally relaxing, no small thanks to Declan.

Who magically appears from the kitchen with two mugs of cider, one of which he hands to me with a grin.

Chuckles' head appears around the corner of a hall-way, sizing up Spritzy, then looking at Andrew and Amanda's enormous, beautiful tree.

"Oh no, you don't," I mutter before sipping cider. Chuckles looks at me, neck twitching, but backs off.

Good.

"All our wires are underground," Andrew answers Dec. "Plus, we have a gas generator and battery backups on the new solar set up," Andrew explains.

"All that?" Dec asks. "I thought you were just remodeling and getting solar hot water for the pool."

"We decided to make the property more resilient," Andrew says, so tersely that Dec gives him a squinty eye.

"And," Amanda adds, yawning, "it was this or buy an underground bunker at a re-purposed nuclear silo in Nebraska."

"Huh?"

Andrew puts his hand over her mouth jokingly. "*Shhhh.*"

She shoves it off and laughs, then stops abruptly, letting her breathing take over, inhaling through her nose. She sets the mug of cider aside with a sour look.

It's clear that this has happened before, because Andrew reaches for a glass of something with bubbles and hands it to her. "Ginger ale?"

Even Declan knows what that means. Eyebrows up, he crosses his arms over his chest and says, "What's really going on, bro?"

The look Andrew and Amanda give each other is the last straw.

"You're pregnant, aren't you?" I challenge Amanda, who doesn't even try to deny it.

"Isn't it wonderful? I'm going to be a grandma!" Pam exclaims. "And Spritzy will be a granddog. Or a grand something." Effusive, excited babbling is so contrary to Pam's normal demeanor that I do a double take to make sure this really *is* Pam.

I turn on Amanda, ready to congratulate her, but somehow the words get hijacked before they come out of my mouth and instead I say, "You sneak! We just had lunch a month ago and you knew then?"

At that exact moment, Ellie wakes up, her face red where it was pressed against Pam's shoulder, the pattern of her sweater imprinted on my baby's chubby cheek. I walk over and take my daughter, unbuttoning my shirt to unclip my bra, latching her on as she sucks happily.

I sink back into my chair and stare at Amanda with great expectation.

"Darn. I have to answer that?"

"Yes! You didn't tell me!"

I overhear Andrew and Declan talking. "That's right, bro. We're pregnant," Andrew crows.

"Pro tip: don't say *we*. Ever. You'll hear about it until the kid is fifty. *We* are never pregnant unless the pregnant woman uses *we*, and even then, pretty sure that's a royal we."

I smirk. He's not wrong.

"I–I really wanted to tell you," Amanda says to me, twisting her hands with worry. "But we agreed we would wait."

"Why? I told you the second I realized!"

"They didn't even tell *me* until this morning," Pam adds. "I opened what I thought would be one of those FitBit contraptions and instead I got a pregnancy test! I like it much better." Pam is grinning like mad, eyes solely on Ellie.

"Why hide it from me?" I can't let this go, can I? Ellie pops off and I sit her up in my lap. She turns my fingers into a teething ring.

Amanda's face is awash with guilt and something... else. "Because–" she starts.

Ding ding ding! Andrew takes a small spoon and taps his glass of wine. Amanda picks up her glass of sparkling water.

"I have an announcement to make," Andrew says with a gleam in his eye.

Uh oh.

I know that gleam.

That is the shining of corneas devoted to competition. The glisten of eyeballs that know they've triumphed.

What could Andrew have possibly done *now* to beat Declan at something?

"Attention!" Even Ellie looks up from her fascinating game of Chew Mommy's Cuticles Off to look at her uncle.

"What's left to tell?" Pam asks, surprised. "We know you two are pregnant."

"*I'm* the pregnant one, thank you very much," Amanda cuts in.

Dec smirks at Andrew, who pales slightly but recovers, grinning at his older brother like a fool.

"And before you ask," she says to me, "I'm thirteen weeks along. We waited until the first trimester was over to be sure. We got the ultrasound, and everyone looks great."

My spidey sense goes off. I look at Amanda.

Who, I swear, is looking at me the way that Andrew is looking at Declan.

I give her a *What's going on?* look.

She smiles like Mona Lisa. Rubs her belly.

And then Andrew holds his glass aloft and calls out:

"To twins!"

:)

THANK you so much for reading about Ellie's first Christmas! To learn more about my future books, release dates, to read excerpts and to get the lowdown on special sales, join my newsletter by visiting my website at jkentauthor.com

LOOKING for a fun book to sink into? Try *Our Options Have Changed*, a spinoff series based on the Shopping series! Shannon, Declan, Andrew, Amanda and more of your favorites from the Shopping series have cameo parts…

HAVING IT ALL IS A FANTASY, **right?**

Chloe Browne knows all about fantasy. Fantasy is her job.

And she's very, very good at what she does.

As director of design for the O Spa chain, a sophisticated women's club that is trending its way into being the Next Big Thing, Chloe's ready to take on the world.

One baby at a time.

Her home study's done, and she's about to adopt, a thirty-something single mother by choice. Who needs to put her life on hold for the right guy when the right baby is waiting for her?

Besides, talk about fantasy.

The right guy?

Pfft. *Right.*

And then in walks Nick Grafton, with those commanding sapphire eyes and wavy blonde hair and a sophisticated mouth that only smiles for her.

He's perfect.

But the last thing Nick wants is to start fresh with a new baby as his college-age kids fly the coop. A single father for more than fifteen years after his wife walked out on her family, Nick finally tastes freedom.

But he likes the taste of Chloe more.

READ AN EXCERPT NOW:

NICK

It takes everything in me not to smile at her.

Everything.

She's a pro. Sophisticated and smooth, gracious and composed, well-versed and well-informed. Chloe Browne moves with a confidence that gives the air in this stuffy conference room an erotic charge. Her dark hair, so smooth it must be soft. A body that doesn't quit. Those brown eyes—tilted slightly, yet paradoxically round. Alert and intelligent, they take in the room.

I'm watching her. It's my job to watch her.

And she's watching me.

Days like this make me love my job.

Her mouth stretches with a delighted precision, as if she were waiting for someone to ask my question. Electricity shoots through me. She's four steps ahead of the rest of us, a chess player who thinks in dimensions, not boards.

One corner of my mouth rebels and rises.

"A great question, Nick." Her lips part slightly. The tip of her tongue slowly touches the edge of her top teeth. Then she gives me a sultry half-grin and says, "Integrating new positions into our body has been so exciting."

I did not imagine that.

Chloe's flushes. "I mean, integrating new *locations* into our body *of work* has been exciting." She clears her throat, squares her shoulders, and continues. "New Orleans is the prototype. O's brand ties in to Anterdec's brand as a luxury option for insiders. People in the know."

"Your maiden voyage." Not smiling is impossible.

Her lip curls up, a mirror image of my own. "This is virgin territory, yes."

Andrew McCormick's eyebrow shoots up as Amanda Warrick's face goes deceptively blank.

"Love the innuendo. Fits nicely with the sensual branding that O cultivates," Andrew says, his words snapping like the sound of buttons on a tailored woman's shirt popping off, as I tear it open in the throes of passion.

Or something like that.

"The Big Easy." Chloe lets that hang in the air, her eyes opening just slightly, then narrowing.

We're playing a game. I don't know the rules, but I sure do like handling the pieces.

"How easy?"

Andrew happens to be drinking from his coffee cup as Amanda asks *that* question, his throat spasming with the kind of hacking that provokes a sympathetic wince from the rest of us.

He glares in response.

At *me*.

There is a moment when you look at a woman for the first time. It's an up or down moment. Thumbs up: yes, I'll sleep with her. Thumbs down: she never enters my consciousness again sexually.

Chloe gets considerably more than a thumb's-worth of *up* from me.

I shift uncomfortably in my chair and try to wrest control back from the strange tension that has infused the room.

This is a business meeting. Branding. My specialty is branding, and on paper, Chloe's spa line has some serious weaknesses. Significant investment in an unproven market means that high risk needs to pay off.

You can't put that kind of trust in just anyone.

"Very easy," Chloe replies, reaching for a clicker and

pulling up a PowerPoint spreadsheet. "Take a look at O Boston. Here's the initial investment. Here's the profit and loss statement."

"Seventy-three percent growth in Year Two?" Andrew lets out a low whistle. My shoulders relax. I had no idea they were tight.

My pants are tighter.

Why am I invested in whether the CEO of Anterdec buys into the O Spa expansion? Until three minutes ago, this was just another pitch.

"Hold on," Amanda interrupts. "That line for marketing and advertising. That figure is impossibly small. Did you forget a digit?"

Andrew gives Amanda a satisfied smirk. "A typo would explain that crazy profitability." He leans back and reaches for his phone. When Andrew McCormick reaches for his phone in a meeting, it's over.

"No."

Chloe's single word rings out like a gunshot.

Andrew's hand freezes.

"That is not a mistake. Word of mouth is our primary form of advertisement."

Andrew makes a grunt I know too well. It's the sound I make when one of my college-age kids asks to borrow the car for a week. In Mexico.

"Isn't that a little too 1990s?"

"Every customer who walks through our doors converts."

"One hundred percent?" Andrew's eyes telescope. "You're certain?"

Click. A new graph appears.

"And each of those customers brings in an average of 3.8 new clients?" Amanda says, reading the slide.

"And that's without paid advertising?" Andrew says skeptically.

Chloe remains unflappable as they read and analyze, talking about O as if she weren't the expert. "Yes. In fact, our business model is counter-intuitive. The more we advertise, the less we sell."

I frown. "That's impossible."

"No, Nick," she says, her voice like velvet and chocolate. "That's O."

"You're saying there's some disconnect between paid ads and foot traffic?" Amanda asks.

"It's lifestyle," I murmur. "The advertising taints the allure. The appeal is in the secrecy. In being told by someone in the know. Women want to be part of the exclusivity, and it's not special if everyone knows about it."

Chloe studies me.

"Like an affair?" Andrew asks. Amanda glares at him.

Chloe pales. It's the first hint of insecurity in her, and it intrigues me. This is a complicated woman.

She recovers quickly. "No. This is nothing like an affair. An affair is a secret because of shame. O is a secret because of *pride*." She squares her shoulders and blinks exactly once, mouth slack and flat, devoid of emotion.

Andrew's voice goes tight. "This is also nothing like any profit and loss statement I've ever read. It's either brilliant or a giant waste of money."

"Brilliant." The word's out of my mouth before I even decide to say it. Our business meeting has lost all pretense of being a corporate affair. Chloe's chest rises and falls rapidly, yet her breath makes no sound.

"You're telling me that Anterdec should make a significant investment in a subsector of the spa industry by trying an unproven and sweeping lifestyle niche—the fourth

185

space—based on a blip in a spreadsheet and promises that word-of-mouth marketing is superior to data analytics we can track on paid ads?" Andrew makes a dismissive noise in the back of his throat.

"No," Chloe says, before I can blurt out the opposite. "We have data analytics as well."

Click.

"Does that column actually say 'sex toys'?" Andrew asks, giving Amanda an arched eyebrow. "You didn't tell me that they—"

"The average client owns 3.2 devices."

"Only 3.2?" Amanda mumbles.

Did Andrew just kick her under the table?

I don't care who is screwing whom at the company, but *knowing* who is screwing whom is strategically important. Catalogue *that.*

"Before they begin patronizing O, that was the figure. After two months of membership, that average increases to 7.9," Chloe explains.

Amanda interrupts her. "Do we sell batteries and chargers on-site at the O spas? If not, we need to."

Andrew raises an eyebrow and tents his hands, index fingers pressed against his lips. "Good point."

What's next? An O Spa porn channel? I almost open my mouth, but stop.

Because they might take me seriously.

"I will add batteries and chargers to our inventory. Great suggestion. All devices purchased on-site," Chloe says to Amanda. "All via careful customer relations management that allows staff to learn their preferences and anticipate their..."

"Kinks?" I ask helpfully.

"*Preferences* is the term I would use," Chloe says, her

voice smooth as silk. "We optimize our device sales. Private label, all made in the USA, no BPA—"

It occurs to me that this is the first professional meeting I've ever attended where the casual discussion of sex toys as a profit-making venture has been a primary topic. Staying cool is key. The CEO acts like we're discussing cars or magazines or lamps.

I wonder what Chloe's *preferences* are.

All 7.9 of them.

Then again, she's hardly average. Bet her number is higher. That mesh corset, after all.

Down, boy.

I raise my hand to a spot above my ear and run a tense hand through my hair. Across the table from me, Andrew McCormick does the same. With great concentration, I return my attention to the screen, where it should be, and not on Chloe Browne's cleavage.

Where it wants to be.

Through the next ten slides, Chloe shows us exactly how brilliant she is, while I struggle to grasp the landscape of the meeting. She walked in here with a fringe idea and a slim chance of convincing Andrew McCormick to invest on the scale she wants.

And now they're talking New Orleans, San Francisco, and—

"Rio would be a great target for 2018," Chloe says, sitting down across from Andrew, tapping the end of a pen against the front of her teeth. "What about Tokyo for 2020?"

"The Olympics!" Andrew and Amanda say at the same time, then laugh.

"We're getting ahead of ourselves," I declare.

"You're not convinced I'm worth taking a chance?"

Chloe asks, her nose twitching with amusement, that curled lip driving me mad.

"You've convinced me," Andrew says, standing and finally looking at his phone. "Nick, make it happen."

"What?"

"Give Chloe whatever she needs."

"Whatever she needs?" I choke out in surprise. Quickly, I recover, face showing no emotion, even if my pulse and half the blood in my body has migrated below my belt and I can't stop wondering what's under that corset. One peek of a nipple is like being given a single sip of Hennessy cognac.

It's great, but you want the whole thing in your mouth eventually.

God help me, her eyes meet mine and her smile widens.

Best. Job. Ever.

"Right. Chloe, why don't you go back to your office for an hour or so, while Nick and Amanda and I hash out some details in the conference room. We'll call you," Andrew says, standing and reaching for her hand. The only hint of emotion in Chloe's face comes from the micro-movements in her eyes. She is pleased.

I want to please her. And not just with Anterdec's money.

In this business setting, she *should* be pleased. Sharp and perceptive, she's turned the meeting around. A green light from Andrew McCormick isn't easy to obtain, and she marched right in here in secret dominatrix lingerie and she did it. I am intrigued and a little spellbound.

Maybe I'm just lightheaded from the lack of blood flow to the brain.

She unmoors me, turning back decades, making me feel like an awkward, uncoordinated teen.

But with a man's appreciation for all that goes into making her *her*.

"Nick?" Andrew's clipped tone makes me realize I'm in my own head. Chloe's standing before me, her nose twitching with amusement, the rest of her face revealing nothing.

"Great presentation," I say, shaking her hand. My eyes float down to her rack.

"It's an eyeful, isn't it?" she jokes.

"Certainly impressive," I confirm. "The *graphs*." I need to dial this down. Andrew's giving me looks that could peel paint. "You give great data."

"I aim to be Good, Giving, and Game."

"Isn't that what Dan Savage says about sex?"

"It applies to business, too."

"A universal set of tools."

She shrugs. "Everyone can have the same tools, Nick. Tool acquisition? Anyone can do that. The real skill is in implementation."

With that, Chloe Browne leaves me speechless, hard as a rock, and the object of my boss's ire.

One hell of a hat trick.

"Coffee?" Andrew's admin, Gina, appears with a smartphone in hand, an app for a local coffee shop open.

Grateful for the save, I give her my order and will myself to think about subjects that deflate. She takes Amanda and Andrew's requests and disappears with quick, nervous steps.

"Didn't know Anterdec added a dating service to our portfolio. Cut it out, Nick," Andrew says with a warning tone as he settles back into his chair.

Amanda snorts.

Catalogue *that*, too.

I say nothing. Eyebrows up, eye contact with my boss, but no words. I don't challenge.

But I don't back down.

"Oh, good Lord," Amanda finally says with a sigh, reaching for Andrew's hand. "*We're* together. Nick can flirt."

Before I can reply, Andrew leads her into the room we're using here at O. I follow, loving the hypocrite he's become in the course of three sentences. We settle around the table, Amanda perched on the edge, Andrew in his chair, me in the chair with the view behind him, the Financial District spread out for us, the ocean stretching behind him as if it were there for his pleasure alone.

It's good to be the king.

"She's good, isn't she?" Andrew says.

And giving and game, apparently.

I give Amanda a look. She shrugs.

"Chloe?" I ask.

"Right. Smart, intuitive, an eye for design, and a great presenter. Gets three layers deeper than anyone in the room ever considered. She's strategic and composed. Perfect face of O."

Her O face sure does come to mind.

Damn it.

"You want to fund her?"

"The RV spa thing seems farfetched, but figures don't lie."

Chloe's figure, bent over the edge of a bed, that sweet ass—

"Nick?" Andrew snaps his fingers. I shake myself like a wet dog.

"Right. How much should I put in her?"

Andrew's jaw grinds, but before he can answer my garbled question, we're interrupted.

Thank God.

"Twelve inches!" Gina exclaims from the doorway.

Timing really is everything.

"What?" Andrew sputters.

She's holding a tray with three enormous white coffee cups in it.

"Twelve inches! The size of these coffees from downstairs. They're so big!" As she hands out the coffee, Amanda stifles a giggle. Sunlight bounces off her ring. A wave of memory pours through me, lightning fast, like a retracting cable that snaps hard at the end, leaving marks.

Simone. Our engagement. Working nights through undergrad to pay for her little diamond chip of a ring...

The same ring she mailed back to me from France, along with her signed divorce papers.

"Jesus, Nick, what is wrong?" Andrew's gone from anger to a furious concern, the irritated worry radiating off of him with a masculine sense that triggers my testosterone, sending me into high alert. We're playing male hormone ping-pong, only without the paddles.

Paddles.

Chloe and a paddle....

"You're not like this. You're the focus man."

"The what?"

"That's what people call you behind your back," Amanda explains cheerfully, her big eyes wide and friendly. They're the color of mink, with lashes so long the bottom layer sticks to the top, making her reach up with a finger and rub.

"People talk about me behind my back? What do they

talk about?"

"Your nickname—pun intended—is Focus Man. Now live up to it," Andrew says sourly.

Damn. I've only been with Anterdec for a year, and so far, so good. After they acquired my firm, my prospects weren't exactly certain. With three kids in college, this needs to last. Just long enough to have an empty nest, and then...

And then no one depends on me. I'm free. Free to pursue whatever I want for the first time in my life.

A flash of mesh corset fills my free mind.

"Focus Man?" I laugh. "I can think of worse names to call me."

We all take a sip of our gigantic coffees and sit in silence for a moment. Andrew types on his computer, drinking more, then looks at me.

"Done. Gina can take care of specifics, but I green-lighted another gO Spa RV and two more locations for new, full-service spas."

"Do I get to help hire the staff?" Amanda asks Andrew with a wink.

"You," he says archly, his voice going low and dark, "are staying at HQ with me."

She gives him a wicked smile.

I miss having a woman smile at me like that.

I wonder if Chloe's free for dinner.

If I'm Focus Man, I can be focused in more ways than one.

GET the rest at *Our Options Have Changed* and immerse yourself in the world of the O Spa, Nick and Chloe, and more....

ABOUT THE AUTHOR

New York Times and USA Today bestselling author Julia Kent writes romantic comedy with an edge. Since 2013, she has sold more than 2 million books, with 4 New York Times bestsellers and more than 19 appearances on the USA Today bestseller list. Her books have been translated into French and German, with more titles releasing in 2018 and 2019.

From billionaires to BBWs to new adult rock stars, Julia finds a sensual, goofy joy in every contemporary romance she writes. Unlike Shannon from Shopping for a Billionaire, she did not meet her husband after dropping her phone in a men's room toilet (and he isn't a billionaire).

She lives in New England with her husband and children in a household where everyone but Julia lacks the gene to change empty toilet paper rolls.

Join her newsletter at http://www.jkentauthor.com

ALSO BY JULIA KENT

Shopping for a Billionaire: The Collection (Parts 1-5 in one bundle, 500 pages!)

- Shopping for a Billionaire 1
- Shopping for a Billionaire 2
- Shopping for a Billionaire 3
- Shopping for a Billionaire 4
- Christmas Shopping for a Billionaire

Shopping for a Billionaire's Fiancée

Shopping for a CEO

Shopping for a Billionaire's Wife

Shopping for a CEO's Fiancée

Shopping for an Heir

Shopping for a Billionaire's Honeymoon

Shopping for a CEO's Wife

Shopping for a Billionaire's Baby

Shopping for a CEO's Honeymoon

Her Billionaires

It's Complicated

Completely Complicated

It's Always Complicated

Random Acts of Crazy

Random Acts of Trust

Random Acts of Fantasy

Random Acts of Hope

Randomly Ever After: Sam and Amy

Random Acts of Love

Random on Tour: Los Angeles

Merry Random Christmas

Random on Tour: Las Vegas

Maliciously Obedient

Suspiciously Obedient

Deliciously Obedient

Our Options Have Changed (with Elisa Reed)

Thank You For Holding (with Elisa Reed)